THE LOVE NEXT TO ME

MONAE NICOLE

UNTITLED

"*I* looked at him as a friend, until I realized I loved him."

1

BROOKLYN

*H*ere I was sitting on the living room floor, crying my eyes out. It wasn't just tears coming down, it was shoulder shaking, and snotty nose crying. My eyes were so puffy, I had to wear my glasses instead of my contacts. My hair was all over the place, and I was exhausted. It seemed like everything I did was never good enough. Pretty soon, my husband, DeWayne would be home soon and I had done absolutely nothing I was supposed to. Ever since we talked on the phone a half-hour ago, I'd been too distraught to get the energy to get everything in the house done, that I needed to do.

He was so angry with me and called me useless; told me that I wasn't good enough to even get the housework done, that he'd been waiting on me to do it for the last couple of days. He acted like I didn't have a job as well. He acted like my job as a dental assistant wasn't real work, even though he had been in the office countless times and saw me work my ass off there. I knew I didn't deserve the way he had been treating me lately. We'd been together for the last seven years and married for the last four years. This was the first time that I had ever forgotten to do the housework.

Well, it wasn't that I forgot, it's just that sometimes I was too tired to do anything. Yesterday, I was too tired to do it, and today, I just felt really sad and didn't want to do it. The problem is, if I didn't do it by the time DeWayne got home, there was going to be problems, and I really don't want to deal with him or his attitude. Lately, his attitude had been out of control. He was always complaining about something, and always trying to argue.

Things had never been this bad. In the beginning of our relationship; DeWayne was thoughtful, caring and loving. This new person was the complete opposite, and I didn't know how much longer I was going to be able to deal with him. Finally getting my tears under control, I got up off the floor to go wash my face and throw my hair in a ponytail and start getting the house together. It's not that the house was even dirty; it just needed a little light cleaning and that's it. DeWayne acted like it was trash everywhere or something. If it was bothering him that much, he could have cleaned up himself, but to avoid any more issues I'd just do it myself.

After straightening up the living room and dining room, I went into the kitchen to get started on dinner. Once I cleaned the chicken and put some BBQ sauce on, I stuck it in the oven. Constantly checking the clock, I tried to hurry and finish making dinner, but I didn't get it done soon enough. As I was preparing the sides, I heard DeWayne enter the house, and I silently prayed that he wouldn't start his mess, but my prayers were unanswered. Immediately, when he walked in the kitchen, I could see the scowl on his face because dinner wasn't ready yet, even though it was cooking now.

"Why the hell dinner isn't done, Brooklyn?" he asked with a slight raise of his voice. That was the first thing out of his mouth. Not hi Brooklyn, how was your day, nothing. It was like he didn't care anymore. He used to come in and kiss me or hug me and ask me how I was doing, then we would talk about how our day was, while we ate dinner. Lately, conversation had been short, unless he was complaining about something, and it was frustrating.

"The food is in the oven, D. I've had a long day, so I got started late. Be a little patient, please. It won't take long." Me telling him that wasn't going to make a difference, it's not like he cared anymore. At least that's what it felt like.

"Brooklyn, I shouldn't have to wait for dinner. It's not like you really do much at work, to be having a long day and not being able to take your responsibilities as a wife, my wife."

I had to pause for a second because just like any other time, he downplayed my job because it was not as lucrative as his. I enjoyed my job, and I made decent money doing it. He felt as though since he can provide for me financially, I shouldn't work and just stay home to do everything for him. That's not how I was raised; my parents instilled in me to never rely on anyone to take care of me. And that's what I was doing. I was planning on enrolling in school to become a dental hygienist, but I hadn't told him yet because I knew he was going to have a problem with that. That would require more of my time and less time to focus on him and his wants. It's something I really wanted to do, so I had to figure out how I could do it without causing more issues in my household.

"You know what, DeWayne, you don't have to act like my job isn't shit because I don't make as much money as you." I clenched my jaw because he was frustrating me already.

4

"Brooke, all you do is hand the dentist a damn instrument, that shit ain't strenuous. And you damn sure don't need to be doing it for money. I told you multiple times, you don't have to work but you want to be on this independent woman bullshit, and if you keep up ya shit, you are really going to be an independent woman," he laughed. Laughed like what he said was funny. I didn't find it amusing at all. Oh, now he wanted to talk like he's going to leave me or something and that was not going to happen. This argument, just like the ones we'd been having for the last couple of nights, was useless. I didn't even care about this dinner, the shit could burn up, for all I cared. In the middle of him yelling about something I didn't care to listen to, I turned away to walk upstairs. When I got on the third step, he asked me about the dinner, and I told his ass to get out of the oven his damn self.

"When is it going to be ready?" he asked before I got too far up the steps.

"Whenever the hell it's done!" I yelled down the steps. I walked into the bedroom, I slammed the door closed and grabbed my iPad, so I could read a little and try to calm myself down. Reading always helped me relax. After reading the first couple of chapters of *Scared of Beautiful by S. Rever*, I calmed down a little but not enough, so I decided to call the only person who could make me feel better, and that was my best friend, Jamir. It was kind of late, and I didn't know if he had company or not, but I knew he would answer the phone for me. He was the one constant in my life.

JAMIR

*T*he sound of my phone ringing woke me out of my sleep. Looking at the screen and seeing it was Brooklyn, made me toss this chick's leg off of me and rush into the bathroom to answer it. It was kind of late for her to be calling me, so immediately, I was on high alert.

"Hey, BB, is everything okay?" BB was a nickname I gave her when we were younger because her maiden name was Bell.

"Hey J, honestly, I'm just getting tired of DeWayne and his attitude. He's been yelling at me more. Lately, he's been thinking I'm his personal damn slave and I'm sick of this shit. Do this, do that. Why isn't my dinner ready, just complaining about anything he can complain about," she cried into the phone. Ever since the day I met her, I hated to see her cry.

"BB, you know how I feel about that nigga and you know I didn't even want you to marry him." I tried my best to get her not to marry his clown ass in the first place. I knew he was a bitch from the first time I met him back in college. He went to a different college from BB and I, and his school was our rivals. Back then, he had this cocky ass attitude and he thought he was a playa, and I didn't want him to hurt BB because she didn't deserve that. When he approached her one night while we were out having dinner, I wasn't happy about it, but she wouldn't listen to me, now we were. I wouldn't hesitate to put my hands on him if she needed me to, and she knew that. That's part of the reason why she really didn't like telling me about the stuff he was doing.

"Do you need me to come over and lay his ass out? Cause you know I've been ready to knock out him since the last time he got buck with you." I caught him before getting loud with her, and the only reason why I didn't put my foot up his ass was because she asked me not to. All I needed was for her to give me the word, and he would be taking a dirt nap, and that's on my momma. I would kill behind BB, and she knew that. I heard her laughing.

"Best friend, thank you for making me laugh, I needed that."

"Well you know, that's part of my job." And that it was. My job was to always protect Brooklyn, and I took pride in that shit.

"What are you doing, though? I know I called you kind of late."

"Nothing, just lying in bed." Even though we were best friends, and I knew all about her fake husband, I tried to keep my extracurricular activities to myself.

"Oh, I know what that means." She laughed.

"That's none of your business, you know that, right?" I questioned.

"You're right. Well, I'm about to go to bed. Thank you for listening. Love you."

"I love you too, big head." I hung up and left the bathroom to get back in the bed.

When I went back in the room, Shanel was sitting up in bed.

"Is everything okay?" she asked with raised eyebrows.

"Yes, everything is cool," I told her. Shanel was someone that I kicked it with from time to time, but I didn't see myself building a future with her. She was five-five, her chestnut brown skin was blemish free and smooth as hell. What got me was her dark brown, mysterious eyes. The minute I met her at work, her eyes just pulled me in. She was beautiful, but there was something that wouldn't allow me to get too close to her, and I couldn't pinpoint what it was. She was cool to be around for the time being, so I dealt with her. For now.

Pulling Shanel closer to me, I laid there, trying to go back to sleep. Unfortunately, sleep wasn't coming easy for me. I just kept tossing and turning. The only thing that was on my mind was Brooklyn and the fact that she was going through the things, she was going through with her husband. She has been there for me at my bad and my worst, since we were eight years old. No matter what happened or who tried to come between our friendship, BB never wavered. I was really getting tired of the way DeWayne treated her. Sometimes, I sat and thought of how things would be if we would have ended up together. There was a situation where we shared a kiss, but nothing went past that. Even though we were drunk,

I still remembered it like it was yesterday. We were coming from one of the parties, and I was walking BB back to her dorm. I had my arm around her shoulders to make sure she didn't fall.

Standing in front of her dorm room door, I couldn't deny the fact that she was so beautiful. I always thought she was, but there was something different about this night. It was like I saw her, really saw her for the first time. Her skin had this glow to it that I never noticed before. I don't know if it was the liquor or what, but something was compelling me to kiss her. I went back and forth with the thought because she was drunk, and I didn't want her to think I was trying to take advantage of that. Plus, I wasn't sure how she would react to it, and I didn't want to make things weird. Watching her lips while she was talking to me, had me wondering what they would feel like on me. After I couldn't take it anymore, I grabbed her by the neck and pulled her close to me. Licking my bottom lip and before she could say anything else, I crashed my lips into hers. Exploring her mouth and it tasting like cherries, had my dick bricking up. Her lips were so soft, and we made love to each other's mouths like it was something we'd been doing for a long time. When she let out a small moan, I knew I had to snap out of it and stop us before we did something we both would regret. Releasing her, she had a shocked expression on her face and rushed inside her room.

The next day, neither one of us said anything about it. I basically blamed it on the alcohol and pushed it to the back of my mind. Thinking back on it, I was too afraid to find out what would happen. What if we didn't make it? That could have potentially ruined our friendship, and her friendship was more important than my feelings for her. Truth be told, I wasn't sure if she really liked me like that anyway. I know for a fact DeWayne didn't deserve her, but sometimes I thought, I may not, either. Oh well, I guess we would never find out.

3

DEWAYNE

I can't believe that not only did Brooklyn not have dinner ready, she also left me down here to get the shit myself. This was some bullshit. Just for that, I was gonna leave my mess right on this table and make her ass clean it up. I sat there in disbelief. On my way up the stairs, I overheard her on the phone with Jamir. I rolled my eyes while trying to listen to their conversation. Rolling my eyes was a bitch move, but I really couldn't stand him. Ever since I met Jamir, I didn't like him. I only tolerated him for the sake of my wife, but I didn't trust him. I saw how he looked at her sometimes, even when no one else did. He would look at her with love in his eyes and not in a friend type of way. Like he thought he had the chance of ever being with her. That wasn't happening because I was never leaving her. He also probably thought I didn't notice that he had a bell tattoo with a B in the middle of it, for her initials. They also got matching tattoos of his football number. That shit wasn't cool, but it was something she had before I met her, so there was nothing I could do about it. I trusted my wife, but that still didn't mean I was comfortable with their friendship. I'd been trying to get her to end her friendship with him altogether, but nothing had worked. Every time he called and asked her to go somewhere, I always found a way to keep her occupied, so she couldn't go. As soon as I heard her getting ready to hang up the phone, I burst through the bedroom door. I came through like I was trying to catch her doing something, but there really wasn't much she could be doing. Throwing her phone down on the bed, she looked up at me like I was crazy.

Since she had an attitude when she left me downstairs, I figured we needed to have a conversation, so I sat down on the edge of the bed to talk to her.

"Brooke, I hate when you don't have the house clean or the dinner ready by the time I get home. You know what I hate even more?" I really was going to try and have a real conversation with her, but the more I thought about her on the phone with Jamir, the angrier I got. Giving her a second to respond; when she only shook her head no, I decided to answer for her. By now I was grinding my teeth, which was something I did when I got angry. Brooklyn must have noticed it too because she scooted back on the bed, trying to get further away from me.

"I really hate when you call Jamir and tell him all of our damn business." I had to tell myself to calm down before things got out of hand.

"Well he is my best friend, who else am I supposed to tell?" she questioned with her tilted to the side.

"You could have called your mom, or you could have talked to me. Hell, you could have told anyone but that nigga!"

I could tell she didn't like what I said because I saw her left eye start to twitch and that was a sure sign of her getting angry. With a head roll, she told me how she could talk to whoever the hell she wanted to, and that I needed to respect her because she was getting tired of the way I talked to her.

"I'm not your child, DeWayne and you're going to stop talking to me like I am!" she yelled.

"Well, if you stop acting like one then I wouldn't talk to you like that!" She got up and grabbed her favorite pillow off the bed and stomped out the room to go to the guest room, I guess.

"Exactly! Like a child!" I yelled as she slammed the door. All I could do was shake my head and get in bed. My attitude was now on a hundred and there was no way, I was going to be able to go to sleep now. Everything was great between us when I was playing football professionally. Brooklyn used to make sure I came to a home cooked meal. She would be dressed in lingerie and heels multiple times a week. Don't get me started on all the sex we used to have. Every single chance we got, we were getting it in. It didn't matter where we were either, we just could not keep our hands off each other. Once I injured my knee and couldn't play anymore, I became depressed. Staying home all day every day had really taken a toll on me. Brooklyn would tell me I was becoming a different man towards her, but I felt like she didn't understand what I was going through. I felt like she wasn't there for me like a wife should have been, and I admit, I did start treating her differently. Really looking back on it, I realized that maybe she was just tired because she had to do everything around the house. Maybe it was a turn-off for her and made her start to act differently towards me. Maybe I took her for granted. I got used to her doing everything and I admit, I got spoiled. Now, I expected her to continue to do everything for me, even though I was capable of doing it myself.

Brooklyn always spoiled me though. I remember one time, I got sick, and she stayed home from work to care for me. She made sure I was fed and took my medicine like I was supposed to. She waited on me and hand and foot. I didn't appreciate it then, like I should have. To be honest, her job wasn't that important, but maybe I should have been more supportive of her.

My wife was so beautiful to me. She didn't have the typical big booty and big titties like I normally liked. Brooklyn was different; she was thin with curly hair that I loved running my fingers through. She has a nice handful of ass, but it was her personality that drew me in. Brooklyn was the type of girl that commanded a room just with her smile, even though she was kind of shy. She was the type of girl that wanted everyone around her to win, and she was supportive. She made sure to tell me when I was wrong, but she also encouraged me to do better. I didn't like the space we were in now. I still remember the day I met her.

We were at this college party at her school, after me and my school kicked their ass in the football game earlier that day. The minute I saw her, I knew I had to have her, but she didn't make it easy for me. I watched her all night and when she was getting ready to leave, I had to shoot my shot.

"Excuse me, sweetheart.," I gently grabbed her wrist, so she wouldn't walk away so easily.

"Do you think you can give me a moment of your time?" She looked down at me holding her wrist, and then looked me in my eye and flat out said no. She wiggled her wrist out of my

grasp and left the party. For the rest of the night, I tried to get some information on her, but nobody would tell me anything. For the next couple of weeks, I looked for her, but couldn't find her. Until one day, I saw her out with that bitch nigga, Jamir, but I wasn't letting him stop me.

"So, Miss Brooklyn, we finally meet again." I knew she was surprised that I found out her name, but I was determined. I gave her my number and waited another two weeks before she called, but ever since then we'd been together.

Brooklyn and I had some good times together, and I was determined to get us back to how we were before all of this.

4

BROOKLYN

The next morning, I was so exhausted that I almost missed my alarm going off. More than likely, DeWayne was still going to be expecting breakfast, but there was no way I was going to get ready, make him breakfast, and make it to work on time. He was on his own this morning, and he was probably going to be pissed, but oh well.

I made it to work right on time and jumped right in, but the minute I sat down, I started falling asleep. It picked back up and before I knew, it was lunch time, and I couldn't be happier. The minute I got to the car, my phone rang, and it was Jamir telling me to look across the parking lot. Sure enough, he was over there leaning on the front of his car, so I made my way over to him. When I got closer to him, he opened his arms, and I stepped right into them. I loved the way his arms felt around me as I inhaled his cologne. Backing away from him, I thought about how good that hug felt and how bad I really needed it.

Shielding my eyes from the sun, I looked up at him and asked him, "What are you doing here?" He smiled at me.

"I'm here to take you to lunch." As soon as he said that, my stomach growled, and I realized I was hungrier than I thought. At first, I had plans on taking a nap and just grabbing a quick sandwich before going back in.

"I know you had a hard night last night, and I just wanted to cheer you up and take your mind off it." He kissed me on my forehead and opened the car door for me. Jamir always treated me like a lady. Something my husband should have been doing but he wasn't. Looking out of the car window, I couldn't believe Jamir was here trying to make my day better, and my punk ass husband still hadn't called and apologized to me or even checked on me to see how I was. I was more so surprised he didn't call me, bitching about me not making breakfast.

We arrived at Olive Garden, which is my favorite place to eat. Pasta and bread were my weakness, and Jamir knew how much I loved the food and strawberry daiquiris there.

For some reason, I couldn't stop wondering who Jamir had in his bed last night. I had to ask him.

"Soo, J, who was in your bed with you last night?" he smirked at me. He took a bite out of his food and just looked at me while he chewed. He was stalling, and I'm not sure why.

"Why do you ask, BB?" he finally asked.

"Because we have been friends forever, and we usually don't keep secrets from each other." I didn't even know why it was bothering me so much, but it was.

Smiling at me, he finally decided to respond, "Don't worry about it, BB, it's nobody. Just worry about what you got going on, I'm good." He winked at me and started laughing.

Rolling my eyes, I told him I was just looking out for him and to be careful because these chicks out here were ruthless. They didn't want nothing but money, and they didn't care how they got it.

After we finished lunch, he took me back to work.

"Thanks J, for taking me to lunch. I hope we can do it again soon. I miss you." I hugged him around his waist.

"You wouldn't miss me if your husband wasn't so much of a bitch ass and trying to keep you away from me."

"Whatever! Don't worry, one day, you will settle down and forget about little ole me," I said, pouting. Honestly, I hoped he didn't find someone else to settle down with.. I'd had this thing for him, but I never told him. That one night in college when we kissed, I figured it was just because he was drunk. The kiss meant everything to me, but I was too afraid to tell him, so I just pretended it didn't happen. I didn't want to ruin our friendship, so I kept it to myself. Once I met DeWayne and fell in love with him after he took my virginity, I pushed my feelings for J to the side. It seemed like now that my husband was being an asshole, those feelings were starting to creep back in. He kissed me on my check and went to get in his car and leave. Walking back inside, my heart was beating out of my chest. Something that I noticed happened when I was around Jamir. DeWayne wanted me to stop being friends with Jamir, but that was something that wasn't going to happen. Jamir was going to be in my life in some capacity, until the day I died. DeWayne was just going to have to get over it.

5

JAMIR

$\mathcal{I}$ couldn't help but to watch Brooklyn walk away. I still couldn't get over the fact that she was married to DeWayne. It was funny to me how he went from an NFL player to basically a nobody, but still acted like he was better than people. As long as I'd known him, he'd been like that. He never humbled himself, and I think that played a part in him getting hurt. Losing everything should have humbled him and made him learn to appreciate Brooklyn, but it didn't. Instead, it made him worse to her. I got back in the car and headed back to the pharmacy I worked at because I was gone for longer than I planned. I was the head pharmacist, so if I came back a little late, it wasn't a big deal, but I was not one to abuse my power. Going into my little office to grab my lab coat, I couldn't wait to get this day over with. Walking out of my office, I looked up and saw Shanel, and she waved and smiled at me. Waving back, I went to start filling prescriptions. I knew it was a bad idea messing with Shanel, but she assured me we wouldn't have any problems, and so far, we hadn't. She never let on that we had any relationship going on, when we are around everyone else. It was pretty slow today, so the other workers went home early, and it was just Shanel and I. Soon, we would be closing up. After filling a few more prescriptions, we closed up the pharmacy and finished doing whatever we had to do to be ready for tomorrow.

Sitting down at my desk, I started thinking about Brooklyn, and I wondered what she was doing so I decided to text her.

ME: ``*WHAT YOU DOING BIG HEAD?*''

BB: ``*Nothing getting ready to head home.*'' She responded with the sad face emoji.

Me: "How was the rest of your day?"

BB: "It wasn't bad, thanks again for lunch."

She didn't have to keep thanking me, but I told her how welcomed she was. If I could do anything to make her day better, I would. Still looking down at my phone, I didn't realize Shanel was standing at my office door.

"What's up?" I put my phone down to give her my undivided attention.

"Nothing, you looked a little stressed. I can do something to help you out." She began walking towards me and taking her lab jacket off and laid it on the chair. She got closer to me and got down on her knees and began trying to pull my dick out. Nobody else was around, so I figured why not.

The minute my dick hit her tonsils; I began losing control.

Grabbing her hair, I started fucking her mouth. "Damn, baby suck that shit." Before I got a chance to cum, she jumped and tried to sit on my dick but without a condom. We weren't on that type of level, so I don't know why she tried it.

"Hold on shorty, you know we don't get down like that." I reached around her to grab a condom out of my desk drawer.

She sucked her teeth, but she knew not to say anything. It was either protected or not at all. She started bouncing on my dick, but I wasn't totally into it. I closed my eyes and the face I saw, almost made cum faster than I wanted to. With my eyes closed; I wasn't with Shanel, I was with BB. Once we were done, she got up to get herself cleaned up. I felt a shift in whatever we had going on. I always enjoyed having sex with her, but this time I felt nothing.

"So, do you want to hang out tonight?" she asked with eagerness in her eyes.

"I'll have to get back to you, I have plans tonight." I saw the disappointment in her face, and I felt bad for lying to her, but I just couldn't entertain her tonight.

"Oh okay, maybe some other time." She turned to walk out the door.

We left out of the door, and I walked her to her car to make sure she got in safely. Once I made it to my car, I got in to head home. I wanted to see what BB was up to, so I called her once my Bluetooth was connected.

"Hey BB, do you have any plans tonight? I was wondering if you wanted to do something." I knew she probably wouldn't be able to go anywhere, but I figured I'd ask anyway.

"You trying to see me twice in one day? What's going on with you?" she giggled.

"Nothing, I just wanted to hang out with my best friend." I really did want to see her again. I missed spending time with her like we used to.

"Mmhmm, something is going on and you're going to tell me sooner or later. Unfortunately, though, I can't make it out tonight," she sadly responded. After reassuring her that I was good, we chatted a little longer before hanging up the phone. I felt a little disappointed that she couldn't hang with me but it's okay. Making it home, I took a shower and got in the bed with thoughts of Brooklyn on my mind.

6

DEWAYNE

*T*oday was a long ass day, and it was finally time to get off of work. Some days, I didn't even know why I worked. Football had always been my passion, but since I couldn't play anymore, I became a sports commentator. I don't particularly care for it, but at least I was still doing something in the sports field. I had enough money to not have to work at all, but what was the point in sitting at home all day? I texted my wife to see what she is up to, and to make sure she was making dinner. Her response immediately pissed me off. She told me she wouldn't be home in time to make dinner because she was going out. She wouldn't tell me exactly where she was going because she knew I would pop up on her ass. Instead of texting her again, I figured I'd call her and tell her how I felt. Listening to the phone ring multiple times and going to voicemail, was making me madder than I already was. Calling back again and getting the voicemail again, I left her a message.

"Instead of worrying about your little boyfriend you should be more concerned about taking care of your husband and making sure I'm satisfied but instead, you want to be out doing whatever the hell you're doing with him!" Before I could say anything else, the voicemail hung up. I tried calling one more time and it went straight to voicemail. I knew at this point, she had me blocked.

Against my better judgement, I scrolled through my phone until I came across Jamir's name. Maybe he could tell me where my wife was. There was no reason why I should be calling another dude to find my wife's whereabouts, but I had no choice right now. The phone rang three times before he finally answered, "What's good?" He knew who it was, so there was no need for the pleasantries.

"Ayo, where is my wife and where the hell do you think you are taking her!"

"My man, you need to mind your own business, obviously your wife didn't want you to know where she is, so I suggest you get off my phone." I hated the cockiness of his tone. I knew I shouldn't have called him anyway. Of course, he wasn't going to tell me. He was trying to make sure he had her to himself, but there was no way he was taking my wife from me. I knew I needed to do better, but it was hard.

"Don't worry, when I see you again it's on!" By now, they both had me fucked up. I'd been wanting to whip his ass anyway, and now this was more of a reason to.

"I highly doubt that, I'll kick you in that bad ass leg you got, and you won't be walking anymore." He laughed in my ear. I just hung up the phone on him. I couldn't sit here and argue with this dude over my wife.

On the drive home, I had hopes that maybe Brooklyn was just messing with me and was really at home, but that hope faded as soon as I didn't see her car in the driveway.

Walking in the house and taking my shoes off, I walked into the kitchen to figure out what I was going to eat. Finding a pizza in the freezer, I took it out to put it in the oven while I went to take a shower.

Feeling the hot water on my body relaxed all the tension I didn't realize I had in my shoulders. It was a long day, and I really did miss my wife. It had been a while since we'd been intimate, and it was starting to catch up to me. I didn't want to cheat on her, but I would be lying if it didn't cross my mind a time or two. I didn't want to be that guy though, so sometimes I would just jerk off in the shower.

Once I handled my business and washed up, I got out the shower so I could get my pizza before it burned in the oven. Throwing on some basketball shorts, I headed back downstairs.

Pulling my pizza out of the oven and grabbing a beer, I went into the living room to eat and tried to find something to watch. Settling on Rhythm and Flow on Netflix, I got comfortable on the couch and tried to enjoy this boring ass pizza. I don't even know why Brooklyn brought these damn pizzas. It didn't even have any toppings on it, just plain ass cheese.

This made me realize that I should have treated her better. If I did, then I would come home to home cooked meals all the time and not be worried about her messing with her best friend.

My views on women weren't so great because of things I'd seen growing up. My father used to verbally and physically abuse my mother and to me, those things were normal. I had never hit Brooklyn, but I was verbally abusive at times. Deep down, I knew it wasn't right, but I didn't know how to stop it. I was afraid she would leave me one day, so I thought if I tried to control her then she would be too afraid to leave, but I felt like I was slowly losing her. I needed to do better, but I felt like it may have been too late.

7

BROOKLYN

It was time to get off of work, and I couldn't be more excited. Luckily, I had some extra clothes in the trunk of my car for cases where I had somewhere to go after work, which never really happened, but still. I grabbed my bag and went to the bathroom, so I could freshen up and change my clothes. I took my ponytail out and fluffed out my curls. I popped a piece of gum in my mouth and applied some fresh lip gloss to make my lips pop. I'd change my shoes once I got to the restaurant. I tried not to drive with heels on, and today's outing called for stilettos. It had been a while since I went anywhere. DeWayne sure didn't take me anywhere anymore, and we definitely hadn't had sex in a while. He had tried a couple of times, but who wanted to be intimate with someone who verbally abused you and called you names. He never told me how beautiful I was anymore. I colored my hair before, and it was like he never even noticed it. It's like he got too comfortable and forgot the things he did to get me, all those years ago. He didn't appreciate my efforts, so I didn't even try anymore.

I changed my mind about going out with Jamir so that gave me an opportunity to get cute, and I was happy about it. I knew DeWayne was going to be pissed because I went out with J and didn't at least leave him dinner, but oh well. Maybe if he learned to treat me better, then I would do those things for him again.

Things changed between us over time, mainly after he got injured and slipped into depression, but even once things got better with him, he still treated me badly. He would do things like call me stupid or dumb, when I would say things he didn't agree with or things he didn't like. He stopped caring about how I felt about things in our relationship. I was supposed to do everything he wanted me to do; no matter if I wanted to or not. He didn't see anything wrong with his actions because in his mind, if he wasn't physically abusing me, then it wasn't a big deal. Him, as well as so many other people, didn't realize that verbal abuse was just as bad or worse than physical abuse. Over time, verbal abuse starts to mess with your self-esteem and confidence. I knew the things he would say weren't true, but when you hear it so much you start to second guess yourself. By the time, he would see the error in his ways, I would be long gone. I should have probably left him by now, but I would when the time was right. Nobody knew the things that went on behind closed doors. Everybody just sees DeWayne Jackson, the football star and now the friendly face they see on their TVs every week. They didn't see DeWayne, the manipulator and abuser. Soon enough, I would be gone and finding better for myself.

Pulling up to the restaurant, I changed my shoes and double-checked my hair and lip gloss before I headed inside.

The minute I spotted Jamir, I headed over to him and he stood up when he noticed me. I noticed a look in his eyes that I don't think I ever noticed before. He looked genuinely happy to see me, but there was also a hint of lust in them. The look passed so fast that I almost missed it, but I didn't. I wasn't going to say anything about it though. Brushing it off, I stepped into his outstretched arms.

"Hey, BB." he kissed me on my cheek before pulling out my chair for me.

"You look beautiful, Brooklyn." The way he said it, sounded a little more sexual than I think he wanted to.

"Thank you." I blushed. I don't know why I felt nervous all of a sudden.

The waitress came over and took our order. Jamir ordered for both of us, and I was not disappointed in his choice. DeWayne would have ordered something totally different from what I would have ordered. Jamir always knew what I wanted without me asking. That made me think of the multiple differences between them. Jamir was always so supportive of the things I wanted to do; whether or not he agreed with it.

I remember back in high school, I wanted to try out for the girls basketball team knowing good and damn well I couldn't play, but that didn't stop Jamir from encouraging me to play. Needless to say, I didn't make the team, but he still got me some vanilla cupcakes that day just for trying out. He encouraged me to pursue my career as a dental hygienist. When we were little, I would try to use different things to clean his teeth, and he really would sit there and let me. I was grateful to have a friend like him. I didn't realize I was smiling, until he interrupted my thoughts.

"What you smiling for?" he asked, smiling himself. I loved to see Jamir smiling, he had a nice smile.

"Oh nothing, just thinking about that time I tried out for the basketball team." I laughed some more.

"Aye, you were brave for trying knowing damn well you couldn't play." He grabbed his glass and took a sip of his drink.

"True, but I wouldn't have done it if you wouldn't have encouraged me," I spoke honestly.

"BB, as long as you're doing something positive with your life, I am going to support you in any way I can. Never forget that." I could see the seriousness in his face.

"Thank you, bestie. So, how has your week been?" By this time, the food came, and it looked so good. Before he got a chance to answer, some girl came to our table and she reached over to hug him. He introduced her as Shanel, and he told her who I was. He also told me that she worked with him, and I wondered if it was the same girl he was with the other night.

8

JAMIR

*T*his wasn't a date between Brooklyn and I but that didn't mean I wanted our time to be interrupted, especially when we barely get to spend time together. Most certainly, not by Shanel either. I didn't need her to pretend things were more than they were between us, in front of Brooklyn. I was just about to tell her how DeWayne called me popping shit and asking about her whereabouts. That shit pissed me off, and it was making me pissed all over again just thinking about it. Noticing Shanel still standing there, was pissing me off too. I could see Brooklyn getting mad about her presence as well. I looked at Shanel and asked her if she needed something else.

With a head roll she responded, "I can see why you weren't interested in spending time with me, you're already on a date." She really had the nerve to be upset. She knew what it was between us and since she wanted to sit there and put on a show, we could end all of this. I didn't do drama, and I for damn sure wasn't going to do it with someone I was not even in a relationship with. I saw Brooklyn gathering her things, so I gave her my attention.

"Oh, this isn't a date," she said to Shanel while standing up.

"BB, where are you going? The food isn't here, and I have something to tell you." I still needed to tell her about DeWayne.

"It's okay J, I have to get home to my husband and your friend here can eat my food." As she said that, Shanel took that moment to sit in my lap.

"Yeah, he'll be fine," Shanel sassed. Brooklyn just rolled her eyes and turned to walk away. I pulled the chair next to me out, so Shanel could sit in it, and I tried to chase after BB, but by the time I got outside, all I saw was the back of her car. I guess I'd go back in here and finish my meal up with Shanel. Walking up to the table, I saw the food had arrived, and Shanel was going in on the food BB ordered, like it was meant for her. All I could do is sit down and try to enjoy my food. This steak and potatoes looked so good my mouth was watering.

"So, who was that?" she questioned with a mouth full of food. I didn't know where she thought she had the right to question me about anything. We weren't together and at this rate, we never would be. One thing, I don't do is unnecessary questioning and trying to start some mess in public and Shanel knew this. To be real, I wasn't even sure where this attitude of hers came from. I know she asked me to come out with her, but that didn't give her the right to interrupt what I had going on.

"Don't worry about who it was, just be lucky I'm letting you sit there and eat that food that was clearly for someone else."

She rolled her eyes, but she didn't say anything else...at least for the moment. That didn't last long though.

As time progressed, I started to notice things about her that were really turning me off and had me questioning why I was dealing with her in the first place. Like, how she was smacking her food and would talk with food in her mouth.

I was just sitting there, trying to enjoy my meal, and she was trying to touch my dick underneath the table. I'm not going to lie, my dick was getting hard, but I really wasn't in the mood for her right now.

"Chill!" I grabbed her hand to remove it from my lap.

She sucked her teeth and crossed her arms over her chest.

I didn't pay her antics any mind, I sat there and ate my food. While sitting there, I thought about BB and was hoping she wasn't going home to no bullshit dealing with her bitch ass husband. I didn't like to see people going through divorces, but I thought she needed to divorce him. I know she wasn't completely happy with him, and he didn't deserve her at all.

"Are you ready to go?" I was so deep in my thoughts, I forgot about Shanel sitting there with an attitude.

"You can go wherever it is you need to go." Her face was one of shock, but I don't know why, I never planned on spending time with her. I needed to be myself tonight. This "date" with Shanel was not planned, nor was it enjoyable. She was only here by default.

"Oh, that's how you doing shit!" She pointed her long ass nails in my face. Comparing her to BB; I noticed a few things about her that I never noticed before. Her clothes were always too tight. Her weave was kind of nappy looking. I think what

34

originally attracted me to her was her fat ass. She was a cute girl, but her attitude was kind of nasty, now that I really paid attention to it. I really needed to cut this situation off with her, but I knew it was probably going to be hard since we worked together. What did I get myself into?

9

DEWAYNE

*C*hecking my watch for the millionth time, it was only nine thirty at night, but that's too late for any wife to be out. Especially my wife. I'd been pacing back and forth so much, I'm surprised I hadn't put a hole in the floor. I didn't know how many times I'd tried calling her and my calls kept going to voicemail. I know she probably had me blocked or had turned her phone off. It was really pissing me off. She was probably out with that nigga, Jamir, and who knows what they could have been doing. Always claiming they were just friends. I didn't believe that shit for nothing, and I never would.

Hearing the sound of the door opening, halted my pacing. The minute I looked up and saw her looking all sexy and shit, sent me in a fit of rage that I couldn't control.

"Where the fuck has your slut ass been? Huh? Probably out fucking that nigga, Jamir!" I was so angry, I had spit flying out of my mouth. The crazy part is that she didn't even look afraid or anything. In fact, she chuckled. She chuckled like this shit was funny, and I really felt like choking the shit out of her, but I knew I couldn't put my hands on her.

"First of all, calm all that hot shit down. Second of all, no, I wasn't out fucking Jamir or nobody for that matter. You wouldn't be so pissed and insecure if you actually paid some attention to me and stopped treating me like I was someone on your payroll and not your wife. I'm not in the mood to fight with you. I'm going to take a shower and go to bed." She spun on her heels to walk away, but I wasn't done talking to her.

"I'm not trying to fight with you either, Brooklyn, but you don't think it's disrespectful for you to be out with another man, while your husband is at home waiting for you and especially looking like that!"

"I wasn't out with just any man, DeWayne. You knew exactly who I was with, and he is my best friend, you know. I'll tell you what's disrespectful though, the way you treat me. Remember, I was the one who did everything for you when you were injured and couldn't do shit for yourself. I took you back and forth to all your doctor appointments. I made sure you had three hot meals a day. I made sure the house was clean. Missing hours at work, so you didn't have to deal with the nurses all day. That wasn't good enough for you though, right. When you slipped into depression, it was me that was there trying to get you out of it. It was me that prayed for you every day, multiple times a day. It was me who tried to get you to talk to someone about how you were feeling, even if it wasn't me. It was me, who helped you get around the house. I took care of you and neglected myself and this is the thanks that I get! Being accused of cheating and being neglected!

You know why I stopped having sex with you?" Her head turned to the side and she looked at me like I was supposed to know the answer. I just shook my head no, so she could continue.

"I stopped having sex with you because I was tired of giving my body to someone who doesn't appreciate me and that doesn't deserve it. I'm sick of this shit!" I can see the tears coming down her face, and I wanted to hug her and tell her I was sorry, but I just couldn't. For one, I knew if I tried to touch her right now, she would probably try to punch me in my face. I also knew that everything she was saying was right. When she turned to walk away this time, I let her go. We both needed to calm down.

I went into the kitchen to pour myself a drink. As I sat there drinking, I thought about everything going on with us, and I knew if I didn't get my shit together soon, I was going to lose my wife. Something had to change and it had to change soon. I didn't know what it was going to take to make things right with her, but I had better figure it out and quickly. I was getting sick just thinking about her leaving me and someone else snatching her up. I sat there and had a couple more drinks before I headed upstairs. When I got upstairs, I saw Brooklyn sitting up, watching TV, and I just stared at her from the doorway. She was so beautiful to me, and I didn't know why I kept messing things up with her. I know, I shouldn't have accused her fucking with Jamir, but I couldn't help it. I hadn't seen her dress like that in a long time, and I got jealous. I was actually jealous of the fact that my wife went out with another man, looking as good she looked. She was only supposed to dress that way for me not anyone else. I probably wouldn't feel so insecure about it, if I treated her better. I knew one thing, I refused to lose her and especially to Jamir. Maybe it was time we talked about going to counseling or something. I missed how we used to be and it was time to fix it.

10

BROOKLYN

I'm sick of men at this point. I'm sick of DeWayne and his bullshit, and I'm sick of Jamir, even though he really didn't do anything wrong. I was really looking forward to a good time with him but that broad Shanel ruined it. She was kind of pretty too; not as pretty as me but not bad looking. I shouldn't have been comparing myself to her. I mean, Jamir was just my best friend, and I had a husband. Who was I fooling; I have more feelings for Jamir than I cared to admit. I mean, he had been the one constant thing in my life besides my parents. No matter what I went through, he was there. When Corey broke my little heart in third grade, Jamir beat him up for me and gave me a lollipop afterwards, to make me feel better. Jamir was always the first person I would call, when I had good or bad news. I just wasn't sure he felt the same way I did, even though he used to always call me wifey. I hated the fact that I had these feelings for him when I shouldn't. I needed to push those feelings way, way down, though. Nothing could ever happen between us.

Seeing DeWayne standing there looking at me, disgusted me. I loved my husband, I really did and he still was fine as hell, but wasn't the same. Everything he did now made my skin crawl. He was rude, his attitude sucked and this new insecurity crap made me mad. Ever since he got injured, he acted like life should only revolve around him. He's healed and even found a new career, but he still acted like an asshole. I knew his job wasn't what he wanted to be doing, but he should have been grateful he had the opportunity he was given. His injury could have been a lot worse. Some people didn't bounce back from that, and they for sure didn't get a good career like he did. He was still involved in the sports world and was still making good money. He really needed to humble himself and appreciate the things he had and not the things he didn't anymore.

I hoped he wouldn't come in here, trying to argue with me because I was over it. I was tired and I just wanted to go to bed. He walked over towards the bed and took his shirt off in the process. I'm not going to lie and say his chest wasn't turning me on because it was, but I wasn't going to tell him that. He still had the body of a football star, and he was still sexy as hell. It's been a while but we still weren't going to have sex, at least not tonight. I thought. If he kept looking at me with love and lust in his eyes, then I may have changed my mind.

Sitting down on the edge of the bed, he grabbed my hand. "Brook, I'm so sorry for how I treated you earlier. Hell, I'm sorry for how I have been treating you, period. I don't know where things went wrong, but I know I'm the blame for it. I love you so much, and I'm afraid of losing you. I think we should go to counseling to make this work."

I was shocked because he never apologized for anything and I couldn't believe he suggested going to counseling. He came from one of those families, where counseling is off limits. That's the problem with a lot of black people and relationships. We feel as though seeking help makes us crazy. It doesn't, sometimes you need that extra person to make you see things you don't see within yourself or each other. Counseling can help, if you go into it with an open mind. You can't go in there with negative thoughts towards it because you will end up with negative results.

He looked at me with sincerity in his eyes, and I wanted to say no, but I couldn't. I owed it to myself to at least give my marriage another shot. DeWayne hadn't always been this bad. I couldn't help but think about the what if's, though. What if it still didn't work out? What if Jamir finally admitted he was in love with me as much as I was in love with him? Would I leave DeWayne for Jamir? All those thoughts are confusing to me, but I had to stop thinking about what could potentially happen and focus on what was happening, and that's my marriage being in a bad state it was in.

"So, are you willing to give us a try?" he pleaded with me.

"Yes, DeWayne. I'll give it a shot. If you're serious about this, you can set up the appointment and let me know when and where." He wanted to do all this, then he was going to have to put in the work.

"I got you baby; I'll handle everything." He smiled at me and looked so happy that I was willing to work on this. I just hoped it wasn't a waste of time. I could see him working on it and being better for a little while but eventually falling back into his old ways. That was one thing I was afraid of. Instead of thinking too much of it, I told myself I was going to go with the flow of things. He kissed me on my forehead and climbed into bed with me.

"Do you mind if I hold you, tonight?" He gave me the puppy dog look he would always give me to get his way, and I couldn't deny that face if I tried. I shook my head yeah, and he climbed in the bed behind me and pulled me close. We laid there and talked about how things used to be with us. It was something we hadn't done in a long time. Before, we would lay in bed for hours just talking about any and everything; our goals and aspirations down to celebrity gossip. It was our way of connecting and to be honest, I missed that. He whispered he loved me, and I hesitated to say it back, but I told him. Maybe he needed to hear it since it's been a while since I said it. I guess, he figured now was a good time to try and have sex because I felt his hand start to rub on my thigh. I wanted to deny him, but I also was a little horny. Between it being a while and seeing Jamir look all good earlier, I needed it. Wait, why was I thinking about Jamir at a time like this?

Feeling DeWayne push me on my back, I let those thoughts of Jamir disappear and focused on my husband.

He began kissing on my neck and down to my breast. They weren't that big, but they were big enough to fit in his mouth. By the time he kissed all the way down to my honey pot, I was soaked.

"Damn, baby you were ready for me?" he spoke right before swiping his tongue between my folds. It felt so good, I had to arch my back off the bed.

It only took a few swipes and a suck before I was coming all over his face. After he came up and wiped his face, he plunged deep inside of me and paused before slow stroking me. The whole time, he whispered how much he loved me and how he was going to fix things. He didn't take long before he came inside of me and we both passed out. It was the first time in a long time that we slept together.

11

JAMIR

inally done eating my food, I was ready to go. This whole situation was irritating as hell. First; Shanel interrupted, then BB left, then Shanel stuck around like this was supposed to be some type of date.

Fake yawning and running my hand over my face, I told Shanel I was about to head out.

"Ok, I'll go with you." She looked at me with anticipation in her eyes, but I was about to burst her bubble.

Taking a deep breath, I responded, "Nah, I'm tired and I'm just gonna go home and crash." I really didn't want to be bothered with her tonight, and I couldn't pretend like I wanted to.

Getting loud, she asked me how I could sleep with her, but not want any real intimacy with her. I got up and threw some money on the table to pay for the meal and tip. Shanel stood up too and was still trying to get me to respond to her.

"Shanel, you don't want to do this; not here and not now."

"Oh, no. We are going to do this now!" she yelled.

I really wasn't trying to hurt her feelings, but she was starting to push my buttons. I could tell her that she was nothing more than a piece of ass to me, but I'm not that type of guy. I tried to handle her with kid gloves but the gloves were close to coming off. She's trying to cause a scene in this restaurant, but I wasn't with it. I turned to walk away from her, and she was right behind.

"You are not going to treat me any way you want. I'm good enough to fuck on, but we can't spend time outside of fucking!" she screamed behind my back. There was some more yelling, but I tuned her out. When she followed me outside and continued her rant, I had enough.

Abruptly stopping I went in, "Listen, Shanel, I can't do this shit with you anymore. We didn't have anything real going on but fucking, that's it, that's all, so I'm not sure where all this anger is coming from. I never made you think we were going to be more than what we are and that's coworkers, who fuck on occasion, but at this point we won't be that either. When you come to work, only talk to me if it concerns work and that's it. Nothing more." I can see the tears pool in her eyes and a part of me felt bad but not enough to apologize. I tried not to take it there, but she left me with no choice.

She slapped the shit out of me before screaming, "Fuck you, Jamir!" and spinning on her heels and walking away.

I regret ever dealing with her, and I hoped she didn't cause any problems at the workplace. If she got out of line even one time, then I was going to fire her. I knew she needed her job, so I wasn't looking forward to doing that, but I would if I had to.

I couldn't believe how this night turned out, and I was over it. When I got in the car, I called Brooklyn to make sure she was good, but she didn't answer the phone. Either she was asleep or just didn't want to answer my calls. Maybe her husband wouldn't let her answer my calls. Just thinking that pissed me off more than I already was. I sent her a text, apologizing about how the night went and asked her if she could find some time soon, to try again.

When I got home, I noticed BB still didn't respond to my text, so I figured she'd just hit me back whenever she got a chance. I needed something to calm my nerves after everything that went down, so I walked over to my bar and poured a shot of Patron. I ended up taking two more shots before I headed upstairs to take a shower and get in bed.

Lying in bed, I couldn't help but think about BB and how things would be if we were together. I would support her dreams, be there for her emotionally, spiritually and physically. I would cook dinner for her everyday and rub her feet when she got off of work. I wanted to be the one she woke up to in the morning and the one she went to sleep with at night. She would never have to question my love for her because I would show her how I felt every single day, for the rest of our lives. It should have been me that she was married to not him. I was in love with her since the first day we met, and I don't know why I never said anything. I felt my eyes getting heavy, so I fell asleep with thoughts of BB on my brain.

"Hey, baby," she purred, walking closer to the bed. She had on this black lingerie set that was sexy as hell. I reached my hand out to help her come closer to me. She leaned down and kissed me and when she tried to walk away, I pulled her back

to me. She just giggled, and I helped her climb on top of me. Leaning down, she kissed me multiple times, and I grabbed her to hold her in place. When I kissed her and she let out a moan, I started rubbing her ass.

Suddenly, I was awakened out of my sleep, right as the dream was getting good. I woke up with my dick in my hand, and I was mad as hell. There was nothing I could do about it, so with an attitude, I turned over and went back to sleep.

12

DEWAYNE

$\mathcal{I}$t had been a week since I mentioned going to counseling with Brooklyn and today was our first session. I was looking forward to it because it could have possibly been the road to us fixing our marriage. Since the beginning of the week, I had been cooking breakfast for Brooklyn before she left for work, and I'd been trying to treat her better.

I was hoping these sessions went fairly easy and it didn't cause us to fight in front of the therapist.

This morning, I woke up a little earlier so I could make a bigger breakfast. Today, we were having waffles, eggs and sausage. I even freshly squeezed some orange juice. I wanted her to see my efforts in trying to make things right.

Yesterday, I grabbed some roses. I set those on the table and made both of our plates before she came down.

When she came into the kitchen, I walked over to her and kissed her lips. She was actually receptive to it and didn't try and push me away. I figured since she was being nice, I'd try and sneak another one in, and she kissed me back.

"Good morning, baby, you look beautiful," I complimented her while pulling her chair out so she could sit down.

She was wearing scrubs like she normally did, but today, she looked more refreshed. I wanted her to know that I still thought she was still beautiful to me.

"Thank you and thank you for breakfast." She smiled and tucked a piece of hair behind her ear.

Sitting down on the opposite side of her, I grabbed her hand so I could bless the food.

For the first few minutes, we sat and ate in a comfortable silence until I reminded her about the session later on.

"Don't worry, I will be there," she assured me.

"Great, have a good day at work." I helped her out the chair and kissed her one more time.

Once she left, I washed all the dishes and cleaned up the kitchen before heading to work, myself.

At work, all I could do was think about this counseling session. I really hoped this thing worked. Brooklyn and I had been at odds for too long, and it was time to get this shit together. I know there was a chance, things may get worse before they get better. We had to lay everything out on the table, and I was a little afraid of how things may turn out.

There were some secrets that could come out that might have made Brooklyn hate me, but I was confident we could push through it...I hoped.

Looking up at the clock, I see the time is creeping by and it was making me anxious. I was ready to go, but that was not going to push the counseling session up any sooner.

Finally, it was time to go, and I was becoming nervous.

I had this fluttery feeling in my stomach and my mouth was becoming dry. This session could go either way and potentially make or break my marriage.

When I parked, I received a text message from Brooklyn letting me know she was running behind, and I prayed that she wasn't bailing out on this. I went inside to let them know that I was here, and that Brooklyn shouldn't be too far behind me.

Seeing Brooke walk through the door, eased some of the tension I was feeling. Only a little bit.

We greeted each other with a quick peck on the lips and waited for someone to call us back.

A few minutes later, Dr. Fowler came and got us and escorted us to her office.

After we all were seated, I grabbed Brooklyn's hand and kissed it. I wanted her to feel as comfortable as possible so she would be able to open up.

"So, what brings you guys in today?" Dr. Fowler jumped right into it.

Clearing my throat and looking over at Brooklyn to see if she wanted me to answer, and when she gave me the go ahead, I got straight to the point.

"Doc, we are here because we lost our way with our marriage, and we are trying to get it back on track." Dr.

Fowler looked at Brooklyn to see if she agreed with what I said, and she shook her head yeah.

She asked Brooklyn where she thought things went wrong, and she answered with no hesitation.

"Once he got injured, he sunk into a deep depression and started treating me like I was a nobody." Her eyes got glossy, and I knew she was trying her best not to let the tears fall.

I squeezed her hand and looked at her apologetically. I really was sorry for her treating her like that, and I was determined to make it right. I didn't expect things to get heavy right out the gate.

"DeWayne, is there anything you want to say to that?"

"Yes, Brooklyn. I am so sorry for treating you like that, and I will do anything in my power to make things work."

Dr. Fowler asked Brooklyn how my apology made her feel and she told her it helped and that she did see me making an effort, and that's all I could ask for right now.

The next thing she asked; I knew was going to cause a problem when I answered it, but it was now or never. Her question was, was there anything that we wanted the other one to change.

Running my hands down my pant legs because they were getting sweaty, I turned towards Brooklyn.

"I want you to end your relationship with Jamir." Her eyes widened and her head turned sideways, but she didn't say anything.

"Who is Jamir?" Dr. Fowler asked, writing something down. I told her about the friendship Brooklyn and Jamir had, and how I didn't trust him around her. I explained how I thought Jamir was really in love with Brooklyn, not just as a friend. I told them how I noticed the look he had in his eyes when he looked at her. The fact that he was always around bothered me. Even the matching tattoos they have are questionable. He also had her initials tattooed on him and neither one of them thought I noticed. Telling her one more time that she needed to end her friendship with Jamir, she just rolled her eyes and turned the other way.

13

BROOKLYN

J was supposed to be at this counseling session a long time ago, but instead I was sitting in my car listening to the numerous messages Jamir left, about why he hadn't heard from me. I felt bad that I had been dodging him. He'd shown up at my job a few times this week, but I pretended not to be there. Ever since the night we went out and that Shanel chick interrupted our dinner, I hadn't talked to him. I knew we would have to talk sooner or later.

Between this situation with Jamir and DeWayne saying he wanted to work things out; it was just too much for me. What I needed was a break from both of them, but I didn't see that happening anytime soon. I did miss Jamir and not talking to him lately, had been really bothering me.

Listening to DeWayne complain about my friendship wasn't anything new. He always had a problem with us being friends, but I knew Jamir first so that was something DeWayne should have dealt with.

For him to say he didn't want me to be friends with him, really hurt me but I tried to not let it show.

"DeWayne, what is it about Jamir you don't like? Or should I say, what is it about our friendship that bothers you?" He never really told me what his problem was with J, and I was curious.

"I feel like you guys have more than a friendship going. I don't like the way he looks at you. He looks like he's in love with you." For some reason, his statement made my heart rate speed up. Could Jamir really be in love with me? I never noticed him looking at me like that before.

"You're full of shit!" My voice came out a little angrier than it should have, causing both DeWayne and the therapist, to look at me weirdly. Like they were shocked by my response.

"Brooklyn, why are you so upset by DeWayne's observation?" Dr. Fowler questioned. She started writing in her little notepad again, and I was wondering what the hell she was writing.

"I'm not upset. It's just...DeWayne knew Jamir was my best friend when we met, and I don't understand why he wants me to stop talking to my only friend outside of him. Jamir has been a pivotal part of my life for a very long time, and I don't think it's fair that we can't be friends anymore to please my husband's insecurities." The tears I was trying to hold back, finally slid down both of my cheeks. DeWayne handed me a tissue, but I could tell he was getting angry about me being so emotional. I could see his nostrils flaring, and his eyes turned cold. He asked for this, so he was going to get whatever needed to be said.

He turned and looked at me with anger, but then it was replaced with concern.

"Yeah, I knew about Jamir from the beginning, but I thought it would have died down and it damn sure was before I knew he had feelings for you. You are a different person when he's around. You become...defiant."

My eyes bulged out of my head because I couldn't believe he said defiant like I was some sort of child.

"It's like you forget about your wifely duties when he's around."

"Wifely duties? Are you..." Dr. Fowler glanced at me.

"Brooklyn, let him finish saying what he has to say and then you can comment on it when he's done. He went on to say how my attitude was different when Jamir was around.

"Jamir is the one constant thing I have had in my life. He took up for me when he didn't even know me. He was there for me when my grandfather died. Everything good or bad; Jamir was there for it. To cheer me on or cheer me up when I needed it. He doesn't talk down to me like you do, DeWayne. He appreciates me and supports my dreams. Not make fun of me because it's not traditional things that most people want to do."

"Brooklyn, do you think you have some type of feelings for Jamir?" It sounded like a question but also like a statement. It was like she knew the answer but wanted me to say it out loud.

"Not...not like that. I mean, I love him but as a friend, nothing more." I hoped I was convincing them because even to me it sounded like a lie.

Dr. Fowler seemed to think that I had some unresolved feelings towards Jamir and of course, I had to deny it but she was right.

"Brooke, all I want is for things to go back to the way they were. When it was me and you against the world baby." He grabbed both of my hands and kissed them.

"I want you to stop treating me like I'm a housewife, when I have a job just like you. We both can do household chores. Together. It shouldn't just be me doing everything. I need your help. He agreed to fix it, but we'd see what happened.

The rest of the session went on with me telling them about how bad DeWayne's injury destroyed me; how it was still destroying our marriage. By the time the session was over, I was exhausted and just wanted to get in bed. I wasn't looking forward to the next one, but if this is going to work, I was gonna have to suck it up and deal with it.

14

JAMIR

*S*lamming my phone down on my desk, I rubbed the back of my next to try and ease some of the tension in it. I had called Brooklyn a million times and probably left a thousand voicemails. No exaggeration. I didn't understand why she wasn't answering my calls. Hell, the least she could do was send me a text message and let me know she was okay. Or at least tell me she wasn't fucking with me anymore. I wouldn't like that, but I'd rather hear that then nothing at all.

Hearing a sound at my office door, I saw Shanel standing there with her arms crossed. I probably should apologize to her but I couldn't, especially not after she slapped the shit out of me the other night. If she knew what was good for her, she would have turned her ass around and went do some work.

I sat at my desk for about an hour or so and every so often, I could see Shanel giving me the evil eye, but I couldn't even entertain her right now.

The only thing on my mind was the fact that Brooklyn still wasn't answering me. The rest of the workday went by slow as hell. Shanel huffing and puffing every five minutes and rolling her eyes at me every time she passed, was making things worse. I was getting a headache worrying about what was going on with Brooklyn.

Five p.m., finally rolled around, and I couldn't wait to get away from Shanel. When I walked past her, she looked like she had something to say, but she kept her mouth shut.

Once I got in my car, I let the window down a little to get some air. That guy D Smoke from that Netflix show just dropped an EP, so I wanted to check that out.

That shit was slapping, and it eased my mind a little. At least temporarily. By the time I got to the fourth song, my phone was ringing through Bluetooth.

Seeing BB's name flash across the screen, made me worry and nervous at the same time. Getting my nerves under control, I answered the phone.

"BB, omg. I was so worried about you. I came by your job multiple times, I've called and texted you so much, I think my phone started calling you on its own. Don't get me started on all the voicemails I have left," I rushed out.

I heard her take a big sigh, and I felt like she was about to say some shit I was not going to like.

"Just drop it on me, BB. I know it's something big." I could imagine her sitting there biting the inside of her cheek. That was always something she did when she was nervous and by the way she was hesitating, I knew she was nervous about something.

Taking a deep breath, she responded, "I have to stop talking to you or at least scale it all the way back, so I don't keep being insensitive to my husband and possibly end my marriage." I felt my heart literally shatter into a million pieces. I couldn't imagine life without BB in it.

"Would that be a bad thing?" I chuckled but deep down, I was serious. She and I both knew he didn't deserve her. Hell, he knew he didn't deserve her, and that's why he was afraid of me being around her. He thought I was going to steal her from him, and I probably could but I wanted her to come to me when she was ready. Trust me when I tell you, she was coming. I just had to be patient.

"Yes, that would be a bad thing, I love my husband, and I have to do what I can to make this work." It sounded like she was trying to convince herself more than she was trying to convince me.

"BB, you're doing this for him, but what about you? What about me? Even if we don't see each other all the time, at least can we talk all the time?" What was I supposed to do without you BB? I was getting sick just thinking about not having her in my life.

"I have to at least try, Jamir. I have to see what life is like without you in it." What she was saying was bullshit and if she didn't have feelings towards me, she wouldn't have to separate herself from me and her husband wouldn't have to worry.

"Brooklyn Monae Bell, do you have feelings for me?" Silence. That's all that was on the phone. Silence. Then she whispered goodbye and hung up.

I just looked at the phone and felt like my world was ending. I was in love with Brooklyn since the day I laid eyes on her, and I should have said something a long time ago. The headache I had earlier was now magnified by ten. I called the only person who knew how I felt about Brooklyn.

"Hey, ma?"

What's the matter, baby?" My mom always knew when something was bothering me.

"Ma, I think I lost BB forever. Her bi… I mean, her husband told her she can't be friends with me anymore." I felt defeated and needed a strong drink and to hopefully wake up from this nightmare.

"I'm sorry baby, but I told you a long time ago to tell her how you feel. All you can do now is move on and pray that everything works out the way it is supposed to."

She was right, there was nothing I could do right now. I talked to my mom for a few more minutes and promised to come to her house for Sunday dinner. Once I got home, I grabbed the whole bottle of Hennessy I had and drank it on the couch until I passed out.

15

DEWAYNE

*N*ow that the first session of counseling was over, I was feeling pretty good. I was finally able to get all that shit about Jamir off my chest, and it felt good. I knew it probably made me look like an insecure bitch, but I didn't care. I was just glad she knew how I felt. She didn't look too happy about my request, but oh well. If she thought this marriage was going to work, then she needed to change some things, as well as I needed to. I could see her on the phone while she sat in her car, and she looked like she's delivering some bad news to someone. I hoped it was Jamir, so we could finally move on to fixing things.

I walked over and knocked on her window. When she rolled it down, I could see the stress on her face, but I chose not to address it. Not yet, anyway.

"Do you think I can take my wife out to dinner?"

"Of course, you can." She smiled at me. I reached in and kissed her cheek and told her to meet me at the restaurant down the street.

Riding to the restaurant, I thought about everything I wanted to say to her.

We pulled up at the same time, so I got out and opened her car door for her. Grabbing her hand, I helped her out of the car and escorted her to the restaurant door. Opening the door for her, we went inside, and I told the hostess we needed a table for two. A second later, she was escorting us to a table, and I pulled the chair out for Brooklyn. Once she was seated, I pushed her chair in and went around to sit across from her. I'd seen Jamir do this for her multiple times and it seemed to make her happy. It's crazy; I had to learn how to properly court my wife, from another guy. I would never admit to that though.

The waitress came and took our order and I thought I was going to die. She was someone I hit a long time ago; in the beginning stages of Brooklyn and I's relationship. I was hoping she didn't say anything. I could see a flash of recognition in her eyes, but it came and went so fast that if you blinked, you missed it. Hopefully, Brooklyn didn't notice. The last thing I needed was someone irrelevant chick causing problems, when things were just getting on track. Luckily, she took our order and left. Let's hope it stayed that way.

"Brooklyn, I just want to apologize for the way I acted at counseling the other day. I really do want to change for you and make this thing work between us. I love you, Brooklyn. I can't wait to work on the homework assignment Dr. Fowler gave us to work on." She wanted us to write down all the reasons why we loved each other and I couldn't wait to do mine because there were so many reasons why I loved

Brooklyn. I noticed she was really quiet, and I hoped she wasn't still mad at me.

"What's wrong, baby?"

"Nothing, DeWayne. I rather not talk about it and ruin our date." One of our biggest problems was communication, so I'd give her a second before I tried to find out what was wrong with her.

"Listen, if this is going to work, we have to be open and honest with each other. So, tell me baby, what's wrong."

Offering me a smile that didn't quite reach her eyes, she told me she was happy that I was trying and how I listened to the therapist, but I could have easily just listened to her. She told me if I would have listened to her a long time ago, we wouldn't have been in this position we were in now. She also voiced how she was upset that I made her cut Jamir off because I wasn't comfortable with it. Honestly, I feel like that was the biggest problem. She then told me that I had successfully caused her to be lonely since I made her cut off her only friend. Her eyes started rapidly blinking, like she was on the verge of tears. She grabbed her pocketbook and ran to the bathroom. I got up to chase her, but I couldn't go in the bathroom with her. Feeling defeated, I walked back to the table with my head down and my hands in my pockets. I saw the waitress at the table, and I was hesitant to sit down alone, but I couldn't do anything else.

"Hey, DeWayne, do you remember me? I see you're still with Brooklyn. Does she know we used to mess around?" She asked that shit like it was recent or something.

"Listen, Carrie. Yes, I remember you. No, my wife doesn't know, and she won't be finding out. Today, or no other day, got that? Now, I suggest you do your job and get away from this table before my wife gets back." I didn't even have to look up, to the look of hurt on her face. Carrie had tried multiple times over the years to get me to continue fucking with her, but it wasn't happening. Not now, not ever. I needed to see what was up with my wife.

16

BROOKLYN

I couldn't get away from DeWayne fast enough. I ran so fast to the bathroom, I almost tripped on my way in there. I couldn't believe I was having a breakdown like this. I hate that I allowed him to dictate my friendship with Jamir. It was an innocent friendship, right? To be honest, I questioned it a few times myself, but we never crossed that line. Well, maybe that one time in college when we kissed, but it was nothing. At least, I don't think it was. I didn't think he thought it was, either. We both were drunk; it just happened, and it never happened again. It did cross my mind a time or two, but I didn't dwell on it.

I noticed how the waitress looked at him, too. He probably thought I didn't notice, but I did. I just chose not to say anything. I remembered seeing her back in college; maybe he used to mess with her back then.

Not realizing I wasn't in the bathroom alone, this woman came up to me and asked if I was okay. I told her I was, as I went to wash my hands. She told me that she was willing to listen if I needed someone to talk to.

I thought about it and what was the harm in talking to a stranger? Someone who has a totally unbiased opinion on all of this.

I went on to tell her everything; from the way DeWayne treated me to everything with Jamir. After a short pause, the lady looked at me and told me that she thought I was in love with Jamir, and I should explore those feelings.

"But, what about my husband? I love him, and we have been together for so long. We have history together." She then tells me that history means nothing when I'm not happy and the way I talked about Jamir seemed like I may be happier with him. It got my wheels turning. Could I really be with Jamir? She told me I needed to follow my heart. The only problem was my heart was going in two different directions right now. My phone dinged and it was a message from DeWayne, asking me if I was okay. I told him I was, and I would meet him at home. I didn't have an appetite anymore, but I hoped he got the food to-go just in case I got hungry later.

"You need to talk to your friend," she mentioned, snapping me from my thoughts. She was right, I couldn't be having all these thoughts and not knowing where Jamir's head was at. If he didn't want me in a lover type of way, could I be okay with that? There were so many thoughts swarming around in my head. I was getting a headache.

"Thank you. Even though I'm more confused than I was when I came in here, I appreciate you listening to me. I really had no one else to talk to about this."

"You're welcome, and I wish you the best." She hugged me and left out the bathroom. I stayed in the bathroom a little longer to get myself together. I wiped my face off and made sure my hair was good and left the bathroom. On the way out, I saw the waitress and she was shooting daggers my way, but I didn't have the energy to deal with her. I noticed DeWayne had left already, so I went to get in my car. I got in my car and with everything on my mind, I sat there and cried again. I didn't feel like going home yet, so I ended up driving around to try and clear my head. After driving around for an hour or so, I found myself sitting outside of Jamir's house. I know I should have probably been home talking to my husband, but I just wasn't ready. I sat there for a minute just staring at his door, contemplating on knocking on the door. What would I even say to him? *Hey Jamir um I'm in love with you and I have been since we were kids.* Nah, I couldn't say that. I didn't know what I would say, but I missed him so much. This was the longest we'd ever gone without speaking to each other, and it was killing me. Maybe the lady in the bathroom was right. Maybe, I should talk to him, but I don't know. DeWayne would be so upset if he knew I was sitting in front of J's house, when I should have been home talking to him. I needed to address the waitress situation, but that wasn't important to me right now. The only thing I could think about was fixing my friendship with Jamir. I couldn't just sit here all night looking at his door, so I finally decided to go knock. Looking in the mirror, I made sure I didn't have raccoon eyes from all that crying, and I applied a fresh coat of lip gloss on my lips before getting out of the car. I locked the doors and made my way up to the door. I hesitated before I knocked because I was nervous. My heart started beating wildly and my palms were sweaty. I ran my hand down the side of my pants before I finally knocked on the door.

17

JAMIR

*A*ll I wanted to do was drink away my pain. I'd been on this couch; getting drunk since BB told me she couldn't be friends with me anymore. My mind must have been playing tricks on me because I see headlights flash from the driveway through my window, and I couldn't imagine who it was. I wasn't expecting anyone. No one comes to my house unannounced, so I thought maybe they were at the wrong house. Taking another shot, I heard someone knock at my door. Getting up, I slipped on whatever the hell was on the floor and now my clothes were wet. I heard the knock again and hoped it wasn't anybody important because I didn't have time to change my clothes.

Opening the door, I was surprised to see BB standing on my doorstep with her arms crossed over her chest, like she was hugging herself. She looked nervous. It baffled me about why she would be nervous. Maybe she was nervous about DeWayne finding out about her coming over here. I'd told her plenty of times, she didn't have to be scared of him. I would kill him and not think twice about it.

I opened the door wider, so she could come in.

"What the hell happened to you?" she asked, brushing past me.

"Nothing, I was drinking. I tripped over the bucket and water spilled on the floor, and I fell into it. Then you knocked on the door, so I couldn't change my clothes and here we are." I realized how drunk I was when my words came out slurred.

"Well, it looks like you've been swimming." She laughed. I didn't.

"What are you doing here? I thought your husband forbade you from talking to me. Hold that thought, let me go change my clothes." I stumbled when I turned around and threw up on the floor. BB helped me to the bathroom and made me sit on the toilet while she ran some bath water for me. After she filled the tub, she helped me get undressed and into the tub. Once I was settled inside, she went to clean up the mess in the living room. I laid back in the tub and thought about the fact that this wasn't the first time we'd been down this road.

Years ago, I got pissy drunk and was stuck at a party, and I had to call BB to pick me up. I ended up throwing up in her car and all over myself. She helped me in the house and helped me in the tub, just like she did last night. BB was my everything and these last few days, I'd been kicking my own ass for not saying anything.

She came back into the bathroom and sat on the side of the tub and began washing me up. Her touch was so gentle. It was comforting. It was safe. I always felt safe around her no matter what state of mind I was in. I knew BB wouldn't let anything bad happen to me.

"Thank you, BB, for always being there for me." I knew all this liquor was going to catch up with me in the morning.

"Jamir, I have to ask you a question, and all I need is a yes or no from you," she said, pulling me from my thoughts. I nodded my head, so she could continue.

"Are you in love with me?" she asked and for a minute, I didn't know what to say. It was now or never. That definitely sobered me up a little.

"Brooklyn Monae, I have loved you from the very beginning, but I was too afraid to say anything. I never wanted you to marry DeWayne, but I was too afraid of you rejecting me, so I swallowed my pride and didn't say anything." She dropped the washcloth and looked at me.

"Jamir, I wouldn't have rejected you. I wish you would have said something before."

I sat all the way up in the tub. "Why wouldn't you have rejected me, BB?"

"Jamir, there's always been something more than just friends between us, but there is nothing we can do about now. I'm married, and I have to try and make my marriage work." She backed away from me and hugged herself. I sobered up real quick and got out of the tub and wrapped my arms around her; wet and all.

"BB, whenever you are ready, I will be right here ready and waiting for you. You deserve better than DeWayne and that better, is me. I know everything about you. I know your favorite color is pink, I know that you can't sleep unless you have fuzzy socks on your feet. I know that for some odd reason, you always wanted to be a dental hygienist. I don't know why, but I support it." I chuckled.

"I know that when you are upset, you bite the inside of your cheek. I know, if you could eat ice cream every day you would, but it upsets your stomach. There is nothing I don't know about you BB, but I'm willing to wait until you're ready. I love you, and I am in love with you, Brooklyn Monae Bell." I gave her a quick peck on the lips and went to put some clothes on; it was getting cold.

"I have to go, Jamir." She rushed towards the door.

"You know where to find me when you're ready, BB." I watched her walk to her car and pull off before I closed the door.

Now that I told her how I felt, the ball was in her court. There were plenty of times I could have told her, but I didn't know how. I didn't want to possibly ruin our friendship, so I kept my mouth shut and now here I was; lonely and potentially without my best friend for good.

5 months later

SINCE THE NIGHT I LAID MY FEELINGS OUT FOR BROOKLYN, IT was like she disappeared. I hadn't heard from her at all. She walked out the door and took a piece of me with her. Things hadn't been the same. All I did was go to work and drink when I came home. Shanel still tried to spend time with me, but I paid her no mind. I didn't have the energy or want to entertain her or any other female, unless it was BB. If things were meant to be with her, then they would be. I was not going to chase her this time. She'd come back when she was ready. I was willing to wait for her, but I didn't know for how long.

18

DEWAYNE

*F*or the last five months, things have been going pretty well for Brooklyn and me. I had started doing more around the house and helping out with things more. I had even implemented weekly date nights, and we are having sex a little more. Not like I would want, but it was better.

I rolled over and watched her sleep for a few minutes. She was laying on her stomach with the covers falling off, so I was able to see her ass, since her nightshirt rose up around her waist. The sight of her exposed ass made me brick up, so I began kissing on her neck. That was a sure way of getting her to wake up and have sex.

While kissing on her neck, I started rubbing on her ass. She slowly turned over and looked at me.

"Good morning baby," I said, climbing on top of her.

"Good morning," she moaned out because I slid into her warm and wet pussy. No matter what was going on with my wife, she had no problem getting wet for me.

Once we were done, I got up to get a washcloth and came back to clean her and myself off. I got back in the bed and cuddled up next to her.

"Bae, when are you going to give me a baby?" All this time we have been together, and we never got pregnant. It made me wonder if she still was taking birth control pills, or she just couldn't have a baby. I wanted a baby by her, but if she couldn't have one, then we would have to explore other options.

"Now, isn't the right time, DeWayne. We just started getting things back on track."

Immediately, I got pissed off. Things had been going great--at least to me they were--and she still acted like nothing was any better.

Lately, she'd been acting like something had been bothering her, but she wouldn't tell me what it was. No matter how much I tried, it was never enough for her. She'd been getting snippy a lot lately.

"What! Why not?" She snatched out of my arms and stomped to the bathroom to take a shower.

"Brooklyn, I thought things were going well between us. Why can't we have a baby, now? Oh, I know what this is about. It's about Ja…"

"Don't you dare say it's about Jamir, when I haven't even talked to him since you told me not to." She got out the shower and grabbed her towel.

"So, what is it, Brooklyn? Mm?" She walked into the bedroom, and I followed behind her. One way or another, she was going to talk to me.

"You want to know what it is, DeWayne!" She hastily grabbed a shirt from the drawer and put it on.

"Even though I pretend to be happy, I'm really not. I love you DeWayne, I do, but we aren't good together."

"Oh, so what you gonna leave me for Jamir? You've probably been fucking him all along!" I yelled.

"And that's the problem, right there. You're worrying about someone that isn't worrying about you. Your insecurities are what's pushing me away, not anyone else but you and your issues. You need to work on that. No matter what I do, you have these thoughts that I'm doing something that I'm not. The shit is driving me crazy! You don't trust me, so why are we together?" She didn't even give me a chance to respond. She just walked out the door and slammed the bedroom door shut. A few minutes later, I heard her slam the front door and get in her car and pull off.

For hours, I just sat on the side of the bed, wondering how we got to this point. I regretted the wrong I did to her and tried coming up with ways to fix it. At this point, I think I lost her for good. She wasn't happy anymore and there was nothing I could do to make her happy again. I would hate to completely lose my wife, but it seemed as though that's what was happening. I couldn't sit here any longer, so I threw some clothes on and headed to the bar that wasn't too far from the house.

Drinking away my troubles didn't seem to be helping. All it did was make me think of Brooklyn.

"Can I get a Long Island iced tea?" I heard a voice next to me, asking the bartender. The voice sounded familiar, but I wasn't sure I wanted to deal with her tonight.

"Hello, DeWayne." I turned to my right, and it was Carrie. Not one to be rude, I spoke to her.

"Hello, Carrie." I turned back around to finish off my drink.

"Is everything okay?" she asked. I didn't want to talk to her, but who else was I going to talk to?

"You know, actually everything is not okay. I fucked up with my wife. I think she's fucking her male best friend, and I may have lost her forever. I didn't appreciate her and now she'll probably go find someone who does." Carrie put her hand on top of mine and rubbed her fingers across my knuckles.

"I'm sorry to hear that, DeWayne. How about I help you take your mind off it for a little while? No strings attached. When the night is over, you can go home and forget you ever saw me." What she said sounded good, but I knew I had no business doing anything with her or anybody that was not my wife. Unfortunately, the liquor kicked in, and I started thinking with my dick instead. "Well lead the way, sweetheart," I told her before taking the last swig of my drink. I followed her outside to her car, and she drove us to her house. The minute she closed the door, she was all over me, and I didn't stop her. The next morning, I woke up with a bad hangover and full of regret.

19

BROOKLYN

*N*o matter how hard I tried, I just could not be happy anymore. I thought ending my friendship with Jamir would help my marriage, but it didn't. Even with Jamir not around, DeWayne was still insecure about him. There was nothing I could do anymore. This marriage had been dead for a while and not even CPR was going to revive it. I was surprised when I came back home, and DeWayne wasn't there. In fact, he never came home, so maybe I should have been the one worrying about him cheating. Maybe he had been all along, since he always accused me. I heard the door open and prepared myself for whatever was about to happen.

"Brooklyn, I'm sooo sorry I didn't come home. I got drunk and slept in my car." He was full of shit. He was definitely drinking because he smelled like alcohol, but he also smelled like some cheap ass perfume. I guess he didn't smell that, but the shit was strong.

"Oh yeah, you and whatever bitch you were with?" He feigned shock like he didn't know what I was talking about.

"I can smell the cheap ass perfume, DeWayne. You know it's crazy that you were always accusing me, but you the one out slinging dick to bitches, huh. You don't even have to answer the shit because I know you were. I have never, not once cheated on you, but I can't say the same for you."

"Baby, I promise this was the first and only time it ever happened. I got drunk and honestly, I don't even remember everything that happened." Did he think that shit was going to make it better? The fact that he couldn't remember, actually made it worse.

"Damn D, did you at least strap up? Or you don't remember that, either!" I shouted so loud, he jumped.

"Um yeah, I think so." He scratched his head. A sure sign that he was lying.

"It doesn't even matter. I want out of this marriage. I'm filing for divorce. You can go be with whoever you were with last night."

"I'm not giving you a divorce, Brooklyn. I don't want to be with anyone else but you. I fucked up, and I promise it will never happen again," he pleaded.

"You're right because I'm done with this. I'm leaving today." I went to grab a suitcase to pack some things, so I could get out of there. I'd stay at a hotel for a few days. I could go to my parents, but I wasn't ready for anybody to know what's going on just yet. I needed a moment to myself.

"Brooke. Baby. You don't think the counseling is working? I think it is." Was he serious right now? He couldn't be.

"If you thought the counseling was working, then you wouldn't have stuck your dick in another bitch! Especially, not the same day you and I had sex. You question me all the time about Jamir, and he isn't even around anymore. You pushed me away, you! Your depression and insecurities did this, DeWayne. Not Jamir."

"I wouldn't be so worried about Jamir, if he didn't have feelings for you and if you didn't have feelings for him. I think that's why you didn't want to have kids by me. It's all because of him!" he shouted.

"You want to know the truth, DeWayne? Yes, I am in love with Jamir, and I have been, but he's not the reason our marriage failed. I pushed those feelings for him deep down and tried. I tried my best to make it work with you, but it's not happening. You asked me about having kids, and I said no. I said no because I'm not happy with you and there was no need to bring a baby into an unhappy situation. It wouldn't be good to bring a baby into this. Can you just give me a divorce?" I picked up my bag, getting ready to leave the house. He told me I'd probably miss him before he missed me but I highly doubted that. I nodded my head at him and left. I finally felt...free. A feeling that I hadn't felt in a long time. I didn't know what was going to happen, but it was time I started living for myself. It was time I did things to make Brooklyn happy; not DeWayne, not Jamir, just Brooklyn. I hoped DeWayne didn't make this too hard and just signed the divorce papers when it was time. Before I left the house, I slid my ring off and put it down on the table by the door.

Once I checked into a hotel room, I hooked my phone up to my speaker. I put Miguel radio on Pandora. I sat on the bed and sipped my wine that was in the room. I thought about everything I went through with DeWayne. We had some good times and bad times. I hated to see things end, but I couldn't pretend anymore. Life was too short to be unhappy. Was Jamir the one for me? Who knows, but I knew DeWayne wasn't. I wished him nothing but the best, but I was looking forward to what life had in store for me next. The first thing I was going to do was enroll in school and become a dental hygienist like I'd been wanting to do.

Pretending to be happy wasn't cutting it anymore. The last time we went to counseling, she told us to be honest and transparent with each other and that's what I was doing, and it felt good.

20

JAMIR

I was in the back filling some prescriptions, when I heard someone calling my name. I looked up and saw DeWayne. He asked me if he could talk to me for a minute, but I told him no because I was busy, so he said he would wait. I didn't think he would, but imagine my surprise when I came outside, and DeWayne was leaning against his car.

"Aye Jamir, are you happy now? My wife is leaving me for your bitch ass!" I had no idea what he was talking about, since I still hadn't talked to BB.

"Man, I don't know what you're talking about. I haven't talked to Brooklyn in months, so I doubt what you're saying is true."

"Nah it's true, she told me she was in love with you, and she was going to leave me," he mentioned, coming closer to me. I backed up a little, not because I was scared, but because I really didn't want to fight him at my job.

"You's a bitch ass nigga!" he yelled, then sucker punched me in my damn mouth. At this point, I was like fuck this job. I punched his ass back, and we started fighting. I heard sirens in the background, and I knew they were coming for us. He should have known not to come here, knowing someone was going to call the police.

"Freeze! Both of you put your hands up!" the cops yelled at us. We both stopped fighting, and they came and handcuffed us while reading us our rights. This was indeed some bullshit. I was going to jail because this man's wife wanted to leave him. It wasn't my fault. I was still shocked she was filing for a divorce. I was wondering why she hadn't called me and told me anything. I guess she needed time to herself and process everything that was going on.

They took us both to the police station and processed us.

After a couple of hours, they let DeWayne go, but I was still sitting there.

The guard finally let me get my phone call, and the only person I could think of calling was BB. I told her everything that happened, and I let her know that DeWayne was already out. She told me that she was on her way, so I hung up and prayed she got here soon and that they would let me out. Before I hung up the phone, I heard her tell me she loved me before she hung up.

While I sat there and waited for her, I thought about how all of this could have been avoided, if we would have admitted our feelings for each other a long time ago. We could have been happily married with children by now. I guess everything happens when it's supposed to and we couldn't rush things. We both had to go through the things we went through, in order to be able to be what we needed to be for each other. Now, I was ready, more than ever, to be what she needed me to be. I just hoped she was finally ready for it.

A few hours later, I was finally being let go. I was hungry and in need of a shower.

The minute I stepped out and saw BB standing there waiting for me, I forgot about everything that happened today.

Walking up to her, I snatched her up in my arms and hugged her like it would be my last time.

"Hi," she shyly said, looking up at me.

"Hi," I said back before tucking a piece of her hair behind her ears. Tonight, she had on her glasses, which she rarely wore, but I thought they made her look sexy as hell.

"About what you said earlier, do you really love me?" I wanted her to repeat it, and I hoped she wasn't just saying it because she thought that's what I wanted to hear.

She blushed before answering me.

"Yes, Jamir. I love you, and I always have." She blessed me with that beautiful ass smile of hers.

"Good, because I love your cute ass, too. You have always been mine; he was just a placeholder until you got it together." She laughed at me before wrapping her arms around me to hug me.

"So, what do we do now?" I know what I wanted to do, but I had to move on her time. Plus, she still was technically married. The sooner he signed those papers, the sooner she would be mine.

"To be honest, Jamir. I just want to get this divorce over with and have my friend back. I would rather take things slow with us because it's been so long since I've been single. We have to make sure this is what we both want."

"I can give you that. I know you are it for me, but I'm willing to play things by your rules. No matter how fast or how slow you want things to go, I'm with you either way. If you need me to be your friend, I got you; if you need me to be your lover, I got you. I'm here for you in whatever capacity you need me in." I meant every word of what I said.

"Well, now I need you to be my eating partner because I'm starving, and I'm sure you are too."

I told her that was cool, but I needed to get my car from the pharmacy and go home to shower and change. As we walked to her car, I filled her in on what happened with DeWayne and told her I would fight him again if I needed to. She laughed and got in the car. Once we got to the pharmacy, I got my car, and she followed me to my house.

Walking behind her to my front door, I couldn't help but look at her ass. I really wanted to take her in there and bend her over my couch. Her leggings made her little booty look plump and soft. I just wanted to touch it, but I kept my thoughts to myself. It had been a minute since I slid up in anything, but I was going to wait until she was ready. I couldn't wait to see what was in store for us.

21

BROOKLYN

I couldn't believe that DeWayne and Jamir had gotten into a fight and got locked up. Of course, I would get him out. I was curious to know how DeWayne was able to get out so fast and Jamir had to wait, especially because DeWayne was the one that started it and he came to Jamir's job. That should have been grounds for something, but I knew Jamir wasn't going to press charges or anything. If anything, he would probably try to fight him again, if he ever saw him. The thought of it had me cracking up.

"What you laughing at?"

"I just can't believe you fools were out here fighting." I was laughing so hard, I had tears coming from my eyes. Two grown ass men fighting for nothing.

"Anyway, so are you really done with him, BB?" He invaded my space and the butterflies in my stomach started swarming. I raked my eyes over his body before I responded, "Yes I am done, I just told you that, Jamir."

"Don't get smart." He gently pushed me.

Cuffing my chin, he pulled my head up so I was looking directly into his eyes. "So, what are we going to do now?" His voice dropped an octave. My heart started beating rapidly against my chest.

"J, I'm not even divorced yet. I think when I am, I need to be myself at least for a little bit. That doesn't change my feelings, but I don't know what it's like to be single. I just need a little time for Brooklyn, you know. Find myself again." No matter how I felt about Jamir, I had to spend some time with myself before I got into another relationship. Not to mention, I still had to actually get a divorce.

"I can respect that. In the meantime, we can still go out together...as friends. I mean, if that's what you want." He gave me a lopsided smile.

"Mmhmm, well for now, let's go get some food and drinks.

Dinner consisted of us eating until we were stuffed and drinking until I was too drunk to drive home.

"BB, you're too drunk to drive home, so I'll take you to my house. I'm sure you probably have some clothes at my house that you can wear. If not, I know you'll just wear one of my shirts or something." He laughed and stood up, so we could leave.

THE NEXT MORNING, I WOKE UP WITH A BANGING HEADACHE, undressed, and not in my own bed. The last thing I remembered was eating and drinking with Jamir. Everything after that, was a blur.

"Good morning, BB." Jamir walked in the room with a tray full of food.

"Shh, why are you so loud?" My voice came out in a whisper.

He chuckled, "I'm not even loud. Yo ass just hungover."

"Did anything happen last night? Why am I naked?"

"Nope, nothing happened. You got drunk, I brought you back here, bathed you and put you in bed," he stated.

Glancing down at the food then back up at him, I thanked him for taking care of me, and the food.

"It's no problem, baby." He kissed my forehead then sat down on the edge of the bed.

"Sit all the way up for me, so I can feed you."

"Oh, this is different. I've never had someone feed me before." *My husband damn sure didn't.* I thought to myself. Looking into his eyes, there was a shift. I always saw Jamir as a really good friend. But right now, the tightness in my stomach made me realize; I loved him.

"There's a first time for everything." He winked.

I could get used to something like this. I was enjoying this side of Jamir. After making sure I was full and giving me some Advil for my headache, Jamir left to go to work, and I went back to sleep. I knew DeWayne was probably calling me, but I didn't want to talk to him right now. I know sooner or later, we would have to talk and come to some type of agreement. I didn't want anything from him; I didn't even want to keep his last name. I just wanted a simple and easy divorce and be done with it. I'd deal with it later, after I took a nap.

. . .

WHEN I WOKE UP HOURS LATER, IT WAS PITCH BLACK IN THE room, and I heard the TV playing in the living room. I got up to go to the bathroom and see where Jamir was.

Finding him on the couch watching TV, I walked over to sit next to him. When I got close, he pulled me down on his lap.

"You feeling any better?" he asked while massaging my scalp.

"Hmm, yes. I feel a lot better." This scalp massage was feeling so good, I moaned.

"Don't start no shit in here, BB." I could feel him get hard underneath me.

"What if I want to start some shit." I smirked and grabbed his face before deeply kissing him. I know, I said I wanted to take things slow; and I was still very much married, but I couldn't help it.

"You not about to control this shit." He lifted us both up off the couch and carried me into his room.

"Are you sure about this?" he asked after he tossed me on the bed. I only shook my head yes because I was too afraid to speak, and I didn't want my voice to come out unsure. I was definitely sure of what I wanted to do right now.

"Well alright, then." He smiled at me as he pulled his shirt off.

Jamir played football in college, so he had a nice body. He still has a six pack, with a defined V leading straight to his slightly curved to left, thick dick. Licking his lips, he walked towards the bed and removed the shirt of his I had on.

"Lay back and relax, baby." Doing as I was told; I scooted a little further on the bed and laid back. Hovering over me, Jamir asked me again if I was sure. I reassured him I was certain, by placing a kiss to his lips.

Deepening the kiss, he used one of his hands to trail down my body; stopping briefly to tweak my nipples, until he found my throbbing and soaked pussy.

"You doing it like that?" Now, he made a trail down the same path his hand had just taken. When he reached my pussy, he whispered, "Pretty, just I thought she would be." Swiping his fat tongue along my folds, he began eating my pussy like it would be his last time.

"Shit," I moaned.

He stuck two fingers in me and continued assaulting my clit. I could feel my impending orgasm, and I knew it was going to be a big one. When he reached my G-spot with his fingers, I couldn't hold it in anymore. He didn't stop until I was screaming his name and releasing on his tongue.

This orgasm was the most powerful, earth-shattering one I had ever felt. DeWayne was orally skilled, but Jamir took it to a new level.

He came up licking his lips before saying, "Damn, that shit was sweet." He licked his lips again.

Hovering over me, Jamir stuck his tongue in my mouth at the same time he slammed into me.

Delivering slow, sensual strokes; he made love to me and it was something I had never experienced before. DeWayne was good in bed, but this with Jamir was different. He looked me in my eyes and told me he loved me before gently biting down on my neck, and I was on the brink of a powerful orgasm. Wrapping my legs around his back to pull him closer, I began bucking my hips until I was creaming on his dick.

"Damn, BB. I need some more of that sweet shit," he moaned against my neck, and I blessed him with another orgasm. When he was pleased that I was satisfied; he picked up speed and slammed into me over and over, until I was scratching his back, screaming his name again, and he released inside of me.

Both spent, trying to catch our breaths, we just laid there in silence for a few minutes.

Reality finally set in that I just fucked my best friend while I was still married. I didn't regret it, but it wasn't right.

"You okay, BB?" My silence must have worried him. "Yes. I'm fine, Jamir. Shocked a little. Well maybe not even shocked because I've wanted this for a while, but not while I'm technically still married." He turned to face me as I was turning to face him.

"Brooklyn, I never want you to do anything you will regret. If I have to wait until you're divorced, best believe the minute the ink dries, I'm on you. Shit, before the ink dries. It was too good for me to not want to slide in that every chance I get."

I just laughed and thought about how things would be with Jamir as my boyfriend and not just my friend. I think with the way our relationship was now, we wouldn't really have any problems.

22

JAMIR

*I*t had been a week since I saw Brooklyn. She said she needed some space to get her thoughts and self together, and I respected that. That didn't stop me from sending her lunch a couple of times during the week.

I missed her, and I wanted to take her out on a date, so I was definitely pulling up on her today.

Today was my day off, so I was going to work out, take her some lunch and hoped she didn't tell me no when I asked her to go to dinner with me.

I didn't feel like going to the gym, so I just worked out a little at home. After showering and getting dressed, I went to *Maggiano's* to get BB and I something to eat for lunch. I knew she wouldn't turn me down if I had Italian food.

I made it to her job a few minutes before she was scheduled for lunch, so she could see me when she came outside.

When she came out, her head was so far into her phone, she didn't see me at first.

Clearing my throat brought her eyes up to look at me. Then she graced me with her beautiful smile.

"Jamir, what are you doing here? And is that *Maggiano's* I smell? She put her nose in the air to inhale.

"Yes, it is, now come on so we can eat at the park up the street." I reached out to grab her hand and helped her get in the car. There was a park close to her job that she liked to go to sometimes, and since it was a nice day, I figured we could eat out there.

Arriving at the park, I got out and helped her out of the car before we walked over to the tables. Once I placed our food and drinks on the table, we sat and began to eat. For a few minutes, we both were quietly enjoying our food until she looked up at me.

"So, what happened to you giving me some space?" Her smirk let me know she was joking.

"Man, fuck space, especially after you gave me a taste of that sweet shit. You lucky I waited this long."

"Well, you're still going to be waiting because he's taking his time signing the papers. I don't want anything from him, so I don't know what the hold up is." I could see the sadness in her eyes. I knew she was ready to end things with him. I for sure, wasn't going to rush her into anything with me, but she wasn't going to be entertaining no other niggas. Brooklyn was mine, and she knew it.

"You know damn well he's not trying to let you go that easy, BB. He fucked up, and he knows it. You were good to him, and he didn't appreciate you, but don't worry; I do, and I always will." I reached over to take her small hand in mine and just held it for a moment.

"So, I know I'm supposed to be giving you some space, but I was wondering if we can go to dinner. You know, as friends." Winking my eye at her, she just laughed and shook her head.

"I mean, I guess we can. Tomorrow would be better for me."

"That's fine, I'll pick you up around seven. That should give you enough time to get off work and relax a little before we go." More than likely, she would get off early and have even more time to get ready. Lord knows she took forever sometimes.

After she agreed, we finished up lunch. I took her back to work, with plans on seeing her tomorrow.

WORK FLEW BY AND BEFORE I KNEW IT, I WAS GETTING ready to pick Brooklyn up for our date. I was taking her to dinner, and we were going to take a salsa dancing lesson afterwards.

When I got home from work, I took a nap then got up and showered and got dressed.

Stuffing my wallet and my phone in my pocket, I grabbed my keys and headed out the door.

The hotel BB was staying at wasn't too far from my house, so it took me no time to get there. I took the elevator up to her room.

When she opened the door, I was happy to see that she was actually ready and damn, she looked good.

"Damn girl, we about to skip dinner. You looking good as fuck right now." She had this red dress on that stopped right above her knees. The top was low cut, and I could see she didn't have a bra on. The black heels she had on, did it for me. Her legs were toned like she'd been running track all her life, and the heels put a little extra lift in her ass. I had to adjust myself because my dick was slowly rising.

After she grabbed her purse, we headed out to my car.

There was a nice steakhouse, so we were going to eat there.

The waitress escorted us to a table, and I pulled out her chair. She smiled at me as I went to take my seat.

"Did I mention how beautiful you look tonight?" She didn't have on her glasses, and she put a little makeup on--not that she needed it--but it looked good on her.

"Yes, but you can tell me again." She blushed.

"I'm gonna tell you that you're beautiful for the rest of our lives," I stated.

The waitress came over and took our order before she got a chance to respond.

"I would appreciate that." Her laughter at her response, caused me to laugh.

We had idle chatter about how both of our work days went until the food came.

23

BROOKLYN

*T*his date with Jamir was going great, and I was glad that I had gone. I was not ready to start an actual relationship with him, but we were still friends. We used to go out to dinner all the time, so this was nothing new.

I felt my phone vibrate a few times, and I imagined it wasn't nobody but DeWayne calling me and unless he signed the divorce papers,there was nothing for us to be talking about. Ignoring the vibrations in my purse, I focused my attention back to Jamir.

"So, are you ever going to tell me about the girl you were with that night? I want to make sure before we fully get into something, you don't have any extra broads lingering around." I didn't need any of his randoms popping up on me, on some woman-to-woman bullshit. Most of the time, he didn't bring anybody around but the few that he did would be insecure and jealous of our relationship, much like DeWayne.

"Oh Shanel, she's nobody. Just some girl that worked at my job, and I kicked it with from time to time. She's definitely nobody for you to be worried about. When you are really ready, I'm gonna be right here, Brooklyn. It's going to be me and you, baby," he stated, and gave me his signature smile.

"Good because I don't need no bullshit J, I had enough with DeWayne, and I don't need any from you. I don't think you would anyway, but I'm just letting you know," I stated, looking him in the eyes.

"I promise, I got you, Brooklyn. You should know that by now," he confirmed. I just nodded my head and smiled. The day Jamir and I met, he told me I would be his wife one day and that no matter what, he would always have my back and he proved that time and time again.

I still remember that day.

I was outside playing with this girl, who I thought was my friend. She was until I got the Barbie Corvette for my birthday, and she was mad she didn't have one. She kept trying to take it from me, and I ended up beating her up. So, she went to get her brother on me. Her brother was older and bigger than both of us, so when he came outside and got in my face, Jamir just so happened to be moving in next door. He saw her brother push me down on the ground, and he came running over to my yard.

"Hey, didn't your mother ever tell you not to hit girls?" Jamir pushed him away from me.

"Nope, cause my momma dead," the boy stated, like he didn't even care.

"Well, someone should have told you that it's not nice, and you won't become a man by hitting girls." The boy punched Jamir, and they began fighting until my mom came outside.

Once they left, Jamir helped me up off the ground and we sat on my porch.

"I'm Jamir, what's your name?"

"Brooklyn," I told him.

"Brooklyn, like in New York? I've been there before." He laughed.

"You're pretty, Brooklyn, and one day you are going to be my wife." He was so sure of it.

"No, I'm not." I rolled my eyes at him.

"You will, but right now we are going to be best friends, and I will never let anybody else do anything to hurt you ever again. Okay?"

"Okay." From that day forward, Jamir has been there.

"J, do you feel like you failed from protecting me from DeWayne?" I know how he is and more than likely he probably felt he didn't fulfill his protector duties, like he thought he should have.

"BB to be honest, yes I do. But at the same time, you are a grown ass woman. I know you loved that nigga, so there was nothing I could do. I knew sooner or later, you would see him as the fuck nigga that he is." I cut my eye at him when he said that.

Laughing he continued, "On some real shit though, I knew it was a matter of time. I'm just glad you left before he got worse."

"You're right, and I'm glad I did, too. I'm also glad that you stayed my friend through it all." He assured me that he would always be there for me.

The rest of the time; we ate, laughed, and drank. It was refreshing, and I needed this opportunity to let my hair down and just chill. We talked about everything during dinner. From politics and this crazy ass president we had, to sports. Conversations with us were never forced, and it seemed as though we always had something to talk about it.

After dinner, he took me salsa dancing. Neither one of us knew how to do that well, but there was someone there giving free lessons, so we joined in. It was fun, and we planned on doing it again. Salsa dancing was sexy, and I'm not going to lie and say that I wasn't getting turned on by watching J move his hips the way he was. We haven't had sex since that night, but I still felt as though we should wait. By the time we were all partied out, it was two o'clock in the morning, and I was tired. He drove me back to the hotel and walked me to my room.

"Thank you, J. I really had a nice time." He stepped closer to me and wrapped a curl around his finger.

"Of course, baby, anytime." He leaned down and kissed me, leaving me with soaked panties.

"Goodnight, BB." He pecked my lips one more time.

"Goodnight, Jamir." I opened the door and went into the shower and went to bed, with a smile on my face.

24

DEWAYNE

*I*t'd been weeks since I'd seen Brooklyn. I'd tried calling her multiple times, left multiple messages; all with no results.

I was hurt when I received the divorce papers, but it was no one's fault but my own. I don't know why I didn't think my actions would eventually push her away. The thing is, no matter what; she probably would never be completely happy with me because she was in love with Jamir. I give her credit for at least trying with me, and I appreciate her for everything she has done for me. I hoped one day we could at least be friends.

After the day she told me she didn't want to do this anymore, I ended up getting drunk and ran into Carrie at the bar again. Between all the shots I had taken, and her ass looking right in the jeans she had on, I ended up taking her back to the house and fucked her all over the place. I knew I was risking Brooklyn coming here and catching me. Even though she wanted a divorce, I didn't want her to come here and catch me with someone else. I knew she'd been coming because I noticed more and more of her stuff being gone. I tried to catch up with her sometimes, but I couldn't.

I continued counseling with Dr. Fowler and came to terms with it all being my fault. Now that I realized that; I was okay with it. Brooklyn and I were never really meant to be, but I think it was an important relationship for both of us. I would have never addressed my real problems, and that was watching my father put my mom through all the things that he did. Now that I was facing my issues, hopefully I could be a better man for someone else that loved me the same. I don't doubt Brooklyn's love for me, but it wasn't wholeheartedly.

I didn't think Carrie was it either. Right now, I was just having fun with her while I continue to better myself. Speaking of Carrie.

"Good morning," she sang, coming out of the bathroom.

She'd been there for the last couple of days.

"Good morning." My response was dry as hell. I was in my feelings about Brooklyn, and I really didn't want Carrie in my space, but she didn't always know how to catch a hint.

She came over and sat down on the bed. She told me her plans for the day and I really didn't care. I just wanted her gone. For now, anyway. Maybe, I'd be in a better mood later. I really didn't have any plans for the day, so I was just gonna lay around the house and watch TV after I worked out.

I took my frustrations out on the punching bag I had in the basement, and it did help a little.

I made myself some lunch and sat down to watch TV.

While watching some random movie on Netflix, I thought about Brooklyn again. I was going to grant her the divorce as well as give her some money, so she could go back to school and buy her a new house. That was the least I could do for putting her through the things I did. I was going to write her a letter and leave it here on the table so whenever she came back and got more of her stuff, she would see it.

I felt better after I finished the letter, so I laid down to take a nap on the couch.

The sound of the door opening, woke me up and surprised me.

"Hello, Brooklyn." She jumped a little, surprised I was here since this was usually my work hours.

"Shit, D, You scared me." She grabbed her chest.

"I'm sorry, Brooklyn. Shit, you scared me." I chuckled and she laughed with me.

"I know you try to come by when I'm not here and usually I'm not, but can we talk for a second?" I brushed my hand over my head.

She looked a little hesitant, but she agreed, and I led her over to the couch.

We both sat down and just looked at each other for a moment. She still looked as beautiful as she did the day we met. It looked like she was doing better than she was the last time. Definitely, less stressed.

"So, how have you been?" I asked her.

"I've been pretty good, how about yourself."

"I'm as good as I can be, given the circumstances. You look well." It pained me to know that I was the one to cause her any pain. That was something I was going to have to deal with for the rest of my life. I could only pray that someone could love me as much as Brooklyn did.

"That's good. I just came by to grab a couple of things, and I'll be out of your way."

"It's okay, you don't have to rush. I just wanted to apologize for everything, and I will sign the divorce papers. I just want you to be happy and hopefully, we can remain friends or at least cordial to each other." I could see the different emotions on her face. On one end, I knew she was happy to be done with me, but at the same time, I know she felt a little sadness because we were never supposed to be in this predicament.

"Thank you. I don't know about being friends right now, but I don't hate you. You will always have a special place in my heart. If I'm ever ready to be friends with you, I know how to find you." She got up from the couch to head upstairs.

"Indeed." I watched her walk up the steps. She left her bag by the door, so I put the letter I wrote in there.

Moments later, she headed back down the stairs, and I helped her get her stuff in the car. Before she got in the car, she kissed me on my lips and told me to take care and drove away from the house and out of my life, taking a piece of me with her.

EPILOGUE

1 YEAR LATER

*I*t had been a year since I drove away from DeWayne after he said he was going to sign the divorce papers, and true to his word, he did.

Later on, that night, I found a letter he wrote to me in my bag. He must have slipped it in my bag when I went to grab some more things. I sat down on the hotel bed and read it.

Dear Brooklyn,

I just wanted you to know how sorry I am for everything I put you through. You never deserved any of it. I let my insecurities get the best of me and pushed you right into the arms of another man. I don't know if you guys are together or not, but I know he will take care of you. If he doesn't, I will kick his ass, lol. Seriously though, I hope you are happy with whoever you end up with and they treat you better than I did. I still continue to see Dr. Fowler because there are things that I had to deal with, and I know that's part of the reason why I treated you the way I did. It's no excuse but that's what it is. I know it's not enough, but I want to pay for your schooling and buy you a house, so you can be comfortable. Again, I'm sorry for everything. Love you forever ~DeWayne

Inside the envelope along with the letter, was the signed divorce papers as well as a check for a million dollars. It was definitely enough for me to go to school and buy myself a three-bedroom house in a nice neighborhood. I was still in school and scheduled to graduate as a dental hygienist next year.

Things were looking up for me. The first six months were a little rough trying to deal with living by myself. I took time to get to know Brooklyn again, not Dewayne's wife or Jamir's best friend. I took time to meditate, I took myself out on dates and sent myself flowers sometimes. It felt good to show myself self-love. Jamir was there through it all, but he always gave me my space. After the first six months, I decided to actually start dating Jamir and things were going great for us. To be honest, not much between us had really changed except intimacy. We still had our dates like we used to but now they usually ended in sex. Sex with Jamir was different. It was mind blowing at times. He took his time learning my body, and he always made sure I was pleased before he was. He would send me flowers every other day. I never had to question his love for me.

We ran into DeWayne one day, and he had a baby on the way. He looked like he was genuinely happy, and I was happy for him. Him and Jamir ended up talking and came to a mutual agreement. I wouldn't say they were friends, but they were friendly to each other.

Today, Jamir was taking me out on a date. I had no clue as to where we were going, but I was looking forward to it, regardless. Only thing I knew was that he was coming to pick me up at ten a.m.

He told me it was going to be an all-day thing, so I should dress comfortably. I put on some distressed jeans with a Dallas Cowboys crop top and some blue and white Air Max sneakers.

At ten a.m. on the dot, he was ringing my doorbell. I grabbed my crossbody bag and headed to open the door.

"Good morning, baby." He leaned in to kiss me.

"Good morning, handsome." I had to kiss him again. I loved kissing his soft, plump lips.

He locked the door for me, and we were on our way.

In the car, he grabbed my hand and kissed it. "Are you ready for our day of adventure?" He winked at me.

"Yes, I'm ready." I was excited; not knowing what we were going to be doing.

The first stop was breakfast at IHOP, where we just talked about the basics. Things like what went on with each other. I mainly talked about my schoolwork.

After breakfast, we headed to this place where we drove go carts and played laser tag, which was fun. They had a couple of arcade games there also, so we played some of those as well.

By the time we were done all that, we went and had dinner at this cute little bistro nearby.

The last stop was a trap and paint event. I always wanted to go to one of those. It was where they played trap music while you sipped your drink of choice and painted a picture. Neither one of us were that great at painting, but it was fun, and we were partying.

I was really enjoying myself. School was harder than I thought it would be, so I needed this break.

Once that was over, we both were beat, so we headed back to my house.

When we got back to my house, I invited him in. He sat down on the couch, so I walked over to him and straddled his lap.

"Thank you for today, Jamir. I had so much fun." I gave him a kiss on his cheek, but he grabbed my face and kissed me deeply. Slipping my tongue in his mouth, I moaned a little. He slid his hand under my shirt and began caressing my breast.

"Take all this shit off," he groaned against my mouth. Just his kiss alone, was causing the flood gates to open.

I stood up to take everything off, and he picked me up and carried me to my room.

I laid down in the middle of the bed, and he told me he had a gift for me. At that moment, all I wanted was some dick, but I'd be patient. He walked over to the bed with a box in his hand. Taking a ring out of the box, he slid it on my finger before saying, "BB since we were eight years old, I knew you were the one for me. This isn't an engagement ring because I know it's too soon for that, but this ring signifies my promise to be there for you whenever you need me. I promise to value your time, your worth, and your heart. I promise to continuously feed your mind, body, and spirit. And when you're ready, I promise to give you all the babies you want after you become my wife. I'm with you forever, baby." His speech brought tears to my eyes, and I didn't think it was possible, but he made my pussy even wetter.

When he slid into me, he asked me, "Are you with me, baby?" He slammed into me.

"Forever," I moaned into his ear.

For the rest of the night, he continued to feed my body.

I never thought Jamir and I would ever be in this space, but I was glad that we were. Who would have thought that my true love was next to me all along?

The End

AFTERWORD

We've come to the end of the road. I hope you enjoyed this story. If you did leave a review on Amazon or Goodreads and recommend it to a friend. I appreciate you for taking the time out to read it.

I want to give a special thank you to my BLP family. You ladies are the absolute best and your encouragement keeps me going on a daily basis. We are sisters for life.

Denishia, thank you for everything you do for me. I really appreciate you.

OTHER TITLES BY MONAE NICOLE

The Love Quest

Follow me on social media: Facebook https://www.
facebook.com/authormonaenicole/

https://www.facebook.com/groups/278291722859991/?ref=share

Instagram: @authormonaenicole

Twitter: @MonaeNicole81

CPSIA information can be obtained
at www.ICGtesting.com
Printed in the USA
LVHW092039061120
670968LV00007B/1165